"Murders make headlines, but discussion of free speech is a more subdued, often obscured topic. The two go hand in hand in this suspenseful novel. A man is found dead and, as is now quite common, disruptive threats are considered protected speech. Detective/professor Kristen Ginelli and colleagues figure out the murder and push university reform. Policy changes can save lives."

—MARY E. HUNT,
co-director, Women's Alliance for Theology, Ethics, and Ritual

"Sometimes everything depends upon the presence of a person who listens. Sometimes it is a listener who makes it possible to speak, and speaking makes it possible to tell the truth, and telling the truth makes it possible to open the doors of yesterday, today, and tomorrow. Here is a story about how that can happen."

—W. DOW EDGERTON,
professor emeritus of ministry, Chicago Theological Seminary

"In *Surfacing*, Susan Thistlethwaite's Kristin Ginelli utilizes her experiences as a friend, former cop, and professor as she brings to light and life the horror and trauma of sexual violence while boldly navigating the systems and structures to help solve a murder she knew her friend might somehow be charged with. This book is not simply a 'who done it' mystery novel, it demonstrates true friendship, compassion, and a willingness to get involved no matter the cost."

—SHARON ELLIS DAVIS,
affiliate professor, McCormick Theological Seminary

"Susan Thistlethwaite's mysteries tell compelling stories that always leave the reader in suspense, but each book also provides an important perspective on a current moral issue—in this case, sexual abuse of young people and how society responds, or fails to respond, to that terrible problem. Her books are fun, but also make the reader think."

—JANET L. MCDAVID,
senior counsel, Hogan Lovells

"Trauma is a pandemic with many causes. In *Surfacing*, the private journey to recovery of a woman traumatized by sexual abuse morphs into the social trauma that tears apart a university community as it deals with a murder and a struggle over the limits of free speech. Through moments of relief with professor Kristin Ginelli, readers can catch their breath and be empowered to name and begin to heal from the traumas they have encountered in this hurting world."

—SHARON RINGE,
professor emerita of New Testament, Wesley Theological Seminary

Surfacing

Surfacing

A Kristin Ginelli Mystery

SUSAN THISTLETHWAITE

RESOURCE *Publications* • Eugene, Oregon

SURFACING
A Kristin Ginelli Mystery

Copyright © 2024 Susan Thistlethwaite. All rights reserved. Except for brief quotations in critical publications or reviews, no part of this book may be reproduced in any manner without prior written permission from the publisher. Write: Permissions, Wipf and Stock Publishers, 199 W. 8th Ave., Suite 3, Eugene, OR 97401.

Resource Publications
An Imprint of Wipf and Stock Publishers
199 W. 8th Ave., Suite 3
Eugene, OR 97401

www.wipfandstock.com

PAPERBACK ISBN: 979-8-3852-1061-9
HARDCOVER ISBN: 979-8-3852-1062-6
EBOOK ISBN: 979-8-3852-1063-3

VERSION NUMBER 07/23/24

Please be aware that this novel includes some fictionalized memories of sexual assault and abuse, as well as accounts of healing in trauma therapy.

Contents

Acknowledgments

I HAVE LEARNED, after writing six novels, that I do not write alone. Dialogue partners are essential to get the story right. Readers also contribute as they write to me indicating their likes and dislikes in the novels they've read. And they clamor, "Where is the next novel?" and that keeps me going.

My main source of support, however, is my family. My husband, Dr. J. Richard Thistlethwaite, Jr. has always made me feel I can do anything. Our sons, James Thistlethwaite, Dr. Bill Thistlethwaite, and Doug Thistlewolf provide me with warmth and affection and the occasional good quotation!

In particular, I would like to thank Dr. Sharon Ringe, New Testament Professor Emerita, Wesley Theological Seminary, Dr. Mary Hunt, feminist theologian and cofounder and codirector of the Women's Alliance for Theology, Ethics, and Ritual (WATER), Janet McDavid, Senior Counsel, Hogan Lovells, Dr. W. Dow Edgerton, Professor of Ministry Emeritus, Chicago Theological Seminary, Dr. Sharon Ellis Davis, Womanist Professor in Pastoral Care, Theology and Ethics, Affiliated Professor, McCormick Theological Seminary, and author of *The Trauma of Sexual and Domestic Violence: Navigating My Way through Individuals, Religion, Policing, and the Courts*, and finally my long time lawyer friend who likes to advise behind the scenes. Any errors in legal or psychological matters in the novel are my own, however.

The settings for my novels are fictional and they, and any characters, bear no resemblance to actual locations or people living or dead. Yes, Chicago is a real city, and yes, the University of Chicago is a real place, but both are types of cities and universities that are simply vehicles for the story. The reference to a law in Illinois that would open a three-year window for adults to report sexual abuse from their pasts is fictional. It is based on a real law that was passed in California.

I would also like to acknowledge those teachers who are now using my books in various kinds of theology and ethics classes. I am touched by this, and I have come to think of this kind of "performative theology" as a new area in the field.

Preface

~

"[Referring to rape] It already is bigger than everything else. It lives in front of me, behind me, next to me, inside me every single day. My schedule is dictated by it, my habits by it, my music by it."

— **Daisy Whitney**, *The Mockingbirds*

It has been a long, hard struggle to gain recognition and treatment for the trauma induced by sexual assault and abuse. The emotional problems created from war were recognized first, though even that was late in coming in human history.

War has dominated the human imagination, of course, but it has been the events of wars themselves and not the human response to them, that have been chronicled.

History, however, can be told through trauma, the emotional response to terrible events both individual and communal. Famine, plagues, war, natural disasters, domestic abuse, and sexual assault all take an enormous toll on the human psyche.

Recognition of the emotional toll, at least of war, began with attempts by physicians to understand the psychological symptoms of veterans from the American Civil War (1861-1865) and the Franco-Prussian War (1870-1871).

World War I (1914-1918), with its widespread carnage, gave rise to the term "Shell Shock." The symptoms of panic and sleeplessness reported by soldiers were thought to have been caused by exposure to the shock waves of the big guns. But soldiers who had not been near that artillery still could have symptoms.

In World War II (1939-1945), the shell shock diagnosis was replaced with "Combat Stress Reaction" or battle fatigue.

But it was the Vietnam conflict (1955-1975) that finally gave rise to the PTSD diagnosis widely used today, though it was a long struggle to get to that point.

Over 3.1 million Americans had been stationed in Vietnam over the course of this long and costly war. Those who survived were increasingly dissatisfied with the poor response of the Veterans Administration to their myriad psychological symptoms. Some got together and helped provide the data to psychiatrists needed to create the diagnosis of Post-Traumatic Stress Disorder.

One psychiatrist they met with was Robert J. Lifton, whose book, *Home from the War: Learning from Vietnam Veterans*, is a powerful critique of militarism and often regarded as the textbook for those working with Vietnam veterans. Lifton's "learning" from listening to the veterans is a real breakthrough itself in psychiatric work.

But PTSD was not widely recognized as a diagnosis of those who had experienced sexual assault and abuse even after Lifton's first work. Another significant figure who also actually listened to survivors of sexual assault and abuse, as well as war and torture, is Judith Herman, and I rely heavily on her work in this novel. (I have also taught her book, *Trauma and Recovery: The Aftermath of Violence—from Domestic Abuse to Political Terror*, many times.)

I believe, as I wrote in *Women's Bodies as Battlefield: Christian Theology and the Global War on Women*, that the widespread violence against women and girls is the world's oldest and longest war. There are many similarities with shooting wars, though each has its own characteristics of damage and destruction. And war includes sexual assault and abuse as a weapon of war, both against those designated "enemies," and among the armed forces against their own.

I strongly urge the reader to read Judith Herman's work as it is so practical and helpful, and I have included it in my discussion questions at the end. We all need to recognize that PTSD is very common in US society.

The National Center for PTSD of the US Department of Veterans affairs estimates that "about 4 of every 100 American men (or 4%) and 10 out every 100 American women (or 10%) will be diagnosed with PTSD in their lifetime."

One message of this novel, and one I have learned from my own life, is that recovery from trauma is possible.

1

~

In order to escape accountability for his crimes, the perpetrator does everything in his power to promote forgetting.

—Judith Lewis Herman, *Trauma and Recovery*

The wide beam of her police issue flashlight picked out the flagstone path. It was nearly covered with the crumpled bodies of the dead leaves of late October.

So much for those damn leaf blowers, campus policewoman Alice Matthews thought grumpily. Noise to wake the dead during the day and then the wind just blows them back at night.

Alice crunched steadily forward, shining her light from the path to the buildings that lined her route. She didn't like the midnight shift, not by a long shot, but her husband Jim had had his hours cut as a trucker, and they needed the extra income. Of course, the campus was more peaceful at midnight without a lot of students getting in the way. At least until Halloween. She'd made sure to not be on the night shift that night. Drunken zombies was what the educated idiots liked. She shook her head. Besides, she liked Trick or Treating with her daughter Shawna. They'd go as a family, dress alike. This year Shawna wanted them all to be rappers. Fiftieth anniversary of rap. Where does she get this at nine-years-old? Alice shook her head. Too fast, growing up too fast.

Suddenly the clouds parted, and a full October moon appeared above the trees, illuminating the campus like a searchlight. She switched off her flashlight. The moonlight picked out the stone turrets of the main campus and spilled down the granite walls. The original university had been modeled on Oxford in England, or so her faculty friend Kristin Ginelli kept whining. "New university in the middle of a young country and who do they ape? The British!"

She smiled a little. Kristin got herself in a twist about the stupidest stuff. Then she sighed. Four more hours. She walked through the archway that led to the next section of the sprawling urban campus where the athletic facilities and the parking garages were located.

No stone castles here. An ultra-modern glass and concrete building rose four stories in the air at one end, tapering to two stories at the other. It was supposed to look like a big sail or something, she'd heard tell, and it housed several swimming pools. It stood just in front of a stand of trees that separated it from a second athletic building where the indoor track and weight rooms were.

She hated pools. The smell nauseated her. But she had to check it, and this stupid sail building had a lot of doors to the outside that she had to cover on her rounds.

She switched on her flashlight again and started toward the rear of the building. She approached the second corner (and this asinine building has like eight "corners," she thought) and stepped into a deep band of shadow broken by a sliver of light from the door directly ahead.

Some idiot leave this door open? She pondered that but she also put her hand not holding the flashlight onto the top of her radio.

She knew this door led directly to the pool area, and sometimes people made a quick exit rather than walk all the way through the locker rooms and out the front.

She opened the door all the way and called out.

"Campus police! Anyone there?"

The short, cinderblock corridor bounced her words back at her but there was no reply.

The chlorine smell got stronger as she moved cautiously down the hall. It was a smell that held horrible memories for her.

No, don't go there, Alice told herself sternly.

The corridor abruptly ended in the pool area, the Olympic size cradle of water chilling her with its hidden depths.

Then she became all cop. There was a body in the pool.

She ran up, switching on the radio automatically to summon assistance.

Then she jerked to a stop. The jets of the pool aerator came on with a sound like a water gun, and the body in the pool rolled over.

She took one look at his face.

She turned and fled, gasping for breath.

She ran outside, headed for the trees, and vomited repeatedly into the dried leaves.

Her head was filled. No, no, no, no, no, no, no. Over and over. Just no. The no's she'd never spoken aloud.

2

~

Every month has an average of 30 days, except the last month of pregnancy, which has approximately 1,333 days.

—Unknown

"It's too quiet," I said to the empty room.

Had the construction guys already stopped for lunch? The new cabinets for the kitchen were being hung this morning, and there should have been more noise.

I looked at my watch. It was barely 11 in the morning.

Had they quit already? I ground my teeth. I was paying the construction firm extra to finish expanding and renovating the kitchen and adding two bedrooms above that extension off the back of our rambling Victorian house. So far, the work had been ahead of schedule, and I kept writing the bonus checks, but we were coming down to the wire. The stupid cabinets had been delayed from the custom woodworking shop.

I nearly screamed in frustration. I was eight months pregnant with twins and on mandatory bedrest. I shouldn't get up to check. I shouldn't. I restlessly moved my legs in the nest of pillows I had on the bed and started to swing them to the side.

No. I stopped moving. Bad for the babies. I could feel them squirming around, probably fighting each other for more space.

I grabbed my cell and called the foreman, Alejandro.

"Yeah?" he answered.

I tamped down my frustration.

"How's it coming with those cabinets?"

"Done," he said and then talked to someone else who was asking him a question.

I clenched my fist. It was like trying to talk to my husband, Dr. Tom Grayson, when he was at the hospital. I'd reach Tom, and then it seemed like half a dozen people would try to talk to him at the same time.

"Listen," Alejandro said. "I gotta go. Plumbers just got here. We get all this hooked up today. No water this afternoon though. You gotta shower or somethin', do it now."

He disconnected.

I thought longingly of soaking in a tub or even taking a shower. Not an option now. Sponge baths. I hated that.

Our golden retriever Molly wandered in. She spent most of her time downstairs with the workers. She had a dog door and could come and go into the backyard. I wished I could.

Earlier, Molly had had a doggy psychotic break caused by my pregnancy. When I'd started to show, she'd torn up newspapers, magazines, and she'd even gone for some books in my study before I'd put a gate in front of them. She had used the torn paper to make nests around the house. Her nipples had swollen, and she'd made sores from licking them. We'd taken her to the vet, and she had been put on doggy tranquilizers. The symptoms had subsided, but it had been chaotic for a while.

My twin boys, now ten, had been very disturbed by that.

"Whadda you mean, she thinks she's pregnant?" my oldest (by a few minutes) Mike had said, grilling me as usual when he was upset. I comforted myself that he'd make a fine lawyer one day.

"Yeah, like that's crazy, Mom," my other son Sam contributed. "She's fixed, right? So, she can't and besides she's not around boy dogs. Well," he paused, "except for Hulk." Sam had the biology of reproduction correct, but Hulk was the teacup poodle who belonged to the son of my colleague. Hulk had a lot of moxie for a five-pound dog, but I didn't think even Hulk could manage that.

I explained she could smell my being pregnant, and it had made her have some fake symptoms of being pregnant herself.

They both had looked angrily at me. There's just so much change children can take without needing to blow off steam. They'd even had some troubles in school, fights with other kids. I'd met with their teachers and then tried to talk to the boys. I'd been stonewalled, big time.

And they'd had a lot of change. They knew I'd captured their father's murderer in the spring, and she had been killed, though not by me. Then I'd married Tom and found out I was pregnant with twins. The summer had been taken over by this big construction project. Even in this enormous Victorian house, we'd needed more space. Expanding the kitchen was a must, and we had to have an extra bedroom for a new nanny. Tom's daughter, Kelly, had graduated and gone to college, though only five blocks away at the university where I taught in the Philosophy and Religion Department. Tom and I had felt it was important that Kelly keep her own bedroom in this house.

I smiled, remembering the unique wedding over the summer of our live-in couple, Carol and Giles. They had helped me with the boys for years, living in an apartment on the top floor. Carol now worked locally as a social worker, and Giles was pounding away in the library on his Ph.D. dissertation. I didn't want to face what it would mean if they moved away.

Giles did all the cooking, and he found the kitchen renovation both disturbing and intriguing. We'd asked for his opinions on the plans, and he'd made very helpful suggestions.

Temporarily, we'd taken a guest bedroom and removed the bed. Folding picnic tables, all the electronic appliances from the gutted kitchen, a small refrigerator and a two-burner cooktop made a temporary kitchen. Giles also used the small kitchen in their apartment. We also got lots of take-out. Dishes were washed in the guest bathroom tub. It was not ideal.

I forced myself to quit obsessing about whether we'd have a functional kitchen when the twins arrived and focused again on the happy memory of Carol's and Giles's wedding. They had hosted a human rights festival on the campus as their wedding venue. It had been a great success. They'd been helped in pulling that off by my former wedding planner, Victoria Layne, and Tom's brother Dr. Dave Grayson, now known as "Uncle Dave." Victoria and Dave were dating, and it seemed kind of serious to me.

So much going on. It often felt like I had been holding this whole rickety structure of our lives together, including my own teaching this fall, just by force of will. And now, I couldn't. Darn this bedrest.

There were some saving graces. I had only one course, thankfully, about the history of religion in America. This was the advanced seminar, not the introductory version, and those majoring in religion or philosophy had to take it.

Our twin girls were due November 11. My plan had been to record a lecture for the week before Thanksgiving, have the babies, give the students two weeks to write their papers, and then finish up the lectures by Winter Break.

No such luck.

I had been put on bedrest two weeks ago. Ten years prior, with the boys, I'd continued running until the 7th month and then walked vigorously right up until the birth.

I sighed, looking over at my computer.

Now I taught using the dreaded Zoom app. I was getting some help from my new colleague, Dr. Nia Zendaya Turner, who was our new appointment in ethics. I'd done some guest lectures for her earlier in the fall for her class "Womanist Ethics and the Social Construction of Whiteness." She was helping me now by giving some lectures on the role of religion in the Civil Rights movements of the 1960's.

In my lectures for Nia, I'd emphasized that many of the 19th and 20th century Christian social reformers had taken their whiteness for granted and even reinforced it. They were reforming conditions "for" African Americans, the poor and non-white immigrants, not "with" them. And it hadn't dawned on them they might ask, "Are these reforms you want?" White privilege in the well-meaning was sometimes harder to confront than the obvious "hurray, I'm white" antics of the Confederate/Nazis currently roaming around in our country.

I looked at my watch.

I was due to start my class by Zoom at 2 pm. Since I'd taught the class several times, I was prepared already. Over-prepared, frankly. I sighed, bored out of my mind. Still, I started to pull the computer toward me thinking to review my notes one more time.

"Mom!"

Tom's daughter Kelly called up the front stairs. She had asked to call me Mom. Her own mother had died in a car accident years before, and she'd come to live with Tom. Back then she'd hated me, but we'd worked it out. The boys had told Tom they already had a dad who'd died, and they'd asked to call him "Pop." Tom and I had been very moved.

"Yeah, up here in my turret," I called back. Family and friends took turns making me lunch. I was grateful, but I hated depending on other people. I always felt like I should do everything by myself. Growing up with physically and emotionally absent parents did that to you. I knew it, but I still felt the effects.

I heard Kelly come up the stairs. She was my height now, a little over 6 feet, and I marveled at how she'd grown into a perfectly gorgeous adult, strong and graceful.

"So, how are you doing?" she asked, dropping her backpack on the floor as she entered. I wondered when kids grew out of that habit.

"I'm okay. Bored out of my mind."

"Ah, I can fix that. I got you the new J.D. Robb," she said, lugging her backpack over to a chair and starting to rummage in it.

I really did like Robb's "In Death" series, and she was incredibly prolific. There were often new books. Robb's detective, Eve Dallas, was a hard-boiled cop with a loving husband. I'd been a cop before I'd quit the force for something I thought would be less violent, like teaching at a university. I had been very surprised to find out just how violent campus life could be.

She located the book in her huge pack and carried it over to me.

"Thanks," I said, placing it on the bed next to me within easy reach.

"So, turkey or ham?" she asked.

"Turkey, I think, but not too much mayo." I had a lot of problems with indigestion these days with two babies pushing up on my esophagus.

She paused in the doorway.

"By the way, did you hear a swim coach was found drowned in the big indoor pool on campus this morning?"

"No. I haven't read the papers," I said, startled. I started to reach for the computer.

"Yeah. They haven't said whether it was an accident, suicide or even murder," she said, watching me carefully.

I read that look correctly.

"Don't worry, Kelly. I'm not going to jump up and go investigate," I said dryly.

"Good. And lunch will be right up," she said and bounded down the stairs.

But I can ask Alice, I thought to myself, planning to call my campus cop friend Alice Matthews after lunch.

Alice will know, I thought.

3

~

You can recognize survivors of abuse by their courage.

—Jeanne McElvancy, ***Healing Insights***

Alice Matthews felt the rigor mortis slowly take over her body until she was almost completely stiff, hands clenched into fists.

Her husband Jim lay snoring next to her in their bed, oblivious.

She heard a metal door shut with a click. The stiffness was reaching her throat. She never had been able to make a sound when it was happening.

"You're so beautiful," the voice said.

No, her mind screamed.

She stood shivering in her wet swimsuit pierced by his hungry eyes.

"You're cold. Let me warm you up," he said coming closer.

No. Soundless.

His touch wasn't warm. Her body shook with cold and then with pain.

Oh, God, her mind yelled. Get up, get out, get away.

She forced her stiff limbs over the side of the bed and stumbled into the hall, down the stairs and out into the cold night.

She hugged herself and rocked back and forth.

Forget it. Forget it. Forget it. Her mind made the words into a prayer. But forgetting wouldn't come.

She looked down at her legs below her nightgown, expecting to see blood trickling down her thighs.

4

~

One thing I'd never thought is that as a full professor teaching a graduate course, I'd be leading a remote class and constantly yelling, "Turn on your microphone!" to someone who clearly couldn't hear me.

—Susan Thistlethwaite on teaching on Zoom

"**How are my girls** this morning?" my husband, Dr. Tom Grayson, asked cheerily as he came out of the closet tying his tie one-handed. Since I knew he could tie surgical knots in a person's chest cavity one-handed, it was not quite the shocking feat I'd once assumed.

Dawn was breaking to the east, and I could now see slivers of light under our quilted bedroom shades that blocked not only light, but also the wind off Lake Michigan. Thank heavens I have a firm rule with the contractors not to start before 8 am. The house was blessedly quiet, and I could even hear Tom speaking without asking him to repeat himself like we did when the hammering and drilling was the worst.

"We're fine, though we were up quite early kicking our little legs up into Mom's stomach," I said lightly. It was true. I'd been up for hours, my abdomen bouncing like a trampoline.

"Well, they're heathy, clearly," Tom said, a little of his soothing doctor voice creeping in. "Ready to get up and use the facilities?"

I nodded, and Tom moved the portable toilet over next to the bed. He helped me get up and sit on it. I'd rented both this portable toilet and a portable sink from a friend who ran a medical supply place with her husband. She and I had been on the Chicago police force together, and we'd quit at the same time. When I called to rent the items we needed, she and I had reiterated how happy we were with our new careers.

As I sat there, Tom went back into the closet, I assumed to get a jacket and to give me some privacy. I finished and continued sitting on the portable toilet until he re-emerged. He had a clean, loose dress in one hand and one of my unstructured suit jackets in the other. I absolutely refused to let students see me on their computers in just the baggy dresses, almost indistinguishable from nightgowns I normally wore, so I shrugged on the loose jackets before I logged on, buttoning them to my neck.

Tom deftly removed the catch basin in the portable toilet and took it into the bathroom. I heard a flush and then water running. He returned with the clean basin, slid it into the track below the toilet seat, closed it and moved it back out of the way.

I envied Tom for getting to wear regular clothes. Every day he put on a pressed shirt (sent out to the cleaners weekly), tie, and a suit or jacket and pants. He immediately changed when he got to the hospital five blocks away and put on a scrub suit and a long white coat. He wore those the whole day and then changed back before coming home. It took seven days for Tom's clothes to even look wrinkled.

When we'd first been living together, I'd pointed out that he could just put on the scrubs and white coat at home and save time. He'd been horrified.

"Walk to work in scrubs?" he had asked incredulously.

You'd think I'd suggested walking there stark naked. Now I too just wanted to be dressed as a regular person. I kept that to myself. I won't whine, I thought for the thousandth time.

"Early case?" I asked when he came out of the closet again.

"I'm taking extra shifts to get time off when the girls are born," he announced. First I'd heard of that.

He came over and sat down carefully on the side of the bed next to me.

"I was a resident when Kelly was born, and I hardly saw her as a baby, well, even as a young child, I guess. I don't want to miss this," he said as he lightly rubbed my stomach. It was still gyrating like a blancmange being carried through a crowded banquet hall by an inexperienced waiter. I reached up and stroked his sandy hair, now lightly sprinkled with grey, out of his eyes. He needed another haircut.

"Don't tire yourself out too much teaching today, okay?" Tom asked, giving my stomach a final pat, and getting up. I didn't reply since what I was thinking was, "Grrrr." I kind of liked the stomach pats, though they made me feel more like an incubator and less like a woman. I'd expected a kiss after I'd stroked his hair, and I hadn't gotten one.

There was a knock on the door. Tom went to open it, and Giles was standing in the hall with a tray with cups, one bowl and a plate with buttered toast.

"Thanks, Giles, but I would have come to get it," Tom said, taking the tray.

"Is no trouble. I made Bori for Kristin, and you know how it is with Bori, Dr. Tom."

Bori was a kind of porridge of Giles's native Senegal, and it could turn to stone if not eaten immediately. Also, it could turn rock hard if you didn't stir it constantly while cooking, something I knew for a fact from having tried to cook Bori.

Tom nodded having encountered rock-hard Bori before.

"I must get to the library now," Giles said, turning and hurrying down the stairs, his flipflops echoing on the wooden treads. Giles was a focused guy. Any faculty would be lucky to get him, I thought, though with the anti-affirmative action mania affecting not only admissions at colleges and universities, but also faculty hires, I was worried.

I realized Tom was at my elbow with a cup of tea in an insulated mug with a lid. Rather like a Tommy Tippy. I tried not to feel infantilized all over again. I was off caffeine entirely now in this delicate pregnancy, though I had promised myself after the girls were born, I'd go back to drinking decaf coffee with a few caffeinated beans thrown in.

Alice Matthews and I had made a pact this past January that she'd quit smoking and I'd quit mainlining nearly a dozen cups of French Roast coffee every day. We'd mostly stuck to our agreement, though I had started drinking decaf before I'd found out I was pregnant. Then I'd even given that up.

Tom put up the bed tray for me and placed the Bori on it with cream and sugar bowls beside it.

He sat down at the small table next to the bed and started munching his toast, sipping real coffee, and scrolling on his phone.

"You know, Kristin, the news stories now say the drowning of that swim coach is being investigated as a suspicious death. I guess this investigation is one you'll have to pass up," he said.

The words were casual and yet I resented them. I had a contract to consult part-time for the campus police and had been instrumental in solving several crimes on campus. I didn't reply but made a mental note to call Alice this morning. I could still consult, I thought sullenly, but I didn't say anything.

I doctored the Bori and took a bite. It was good as usual, it just wasn't coffee and toast. Then one of the babies kicked hard, and the bed tray over my nonexistent lap rocked. I steadied it and started consuming the Bori in earnest. I remembered trying to eat while having twin newborns, and I figured I'd better practice eating fast. I looked over at Tom. Talk about someone who ate quickly. He was already finished and putting his suit jacket on.

Molly walked in having smelled the food, and the boys were right behind her.

"Hi, Mom, hi, Pop!" they chorused. They had just gotten out of bed, it seemed, and their dark brown hair was tousled and their pajamas rumpled. I caught my breath. There were these brief times when they looked so much like their father Marco, it hurt my heart.

Their inflection when they said "Pop" was always a tiny bit tentative, but it was disappearing as they said it more often. Tom wisely took no note of that.

"Hi, guys. Listen, I have to go to the hospital. Take care of your mom, okay?"

"Of course, we will," Mike said seriously.

"Yeah!" Sam affirmed.

They headed for the bed, and Tom rescued the bed tray right before they jumped up on to the mattress. Molly made a move to do the same, but Mike said "No, Molly!" sharply, and she stopped. Mike had never before talked to her like that. Her doggy face actually looked hurt. Their stress was just below the surface. I have to remember that, I cautioned myself.

Finally, everyone was out the front door. I had been assured by Carol that Victoria, our former wedding planner, would be by later this morning and work on her computer from our library. She'd fix my lunch.

I was glad she was the one coming. When I asked her, she'd wash my hair and blow it dry nicely. I thought I'd request that today. Yesterday in the online class I'd thought my long hair, even pulled back into a bun at the nape of my neck, had looked ratty. My face was also a little bloated and that didn't help with a professional look.

I agreed in principle that having an adult here while I was gestating so precariously was a good idea. But I hated people taking care of me, and I knew they were all talking to each other about their schedules and who could do what. They were not talking to me. Just like Tom deciding he'd take extra shifts to get time off. I'd have said yes, but I'd have liked to have been consulted. Victoria was the exception. She actually asked me what I'd like.

Two more weeks, I thought, and I picked up my cell phone to call Alice. She was on my speed dial, but it went straight to voicemail.

"It's me," I said. "Call me."

Then I pulled my computer over so I could review the notes for the class later today, but the corner of the device dislodged the new mystery novel Kelly had brought me from where it had gotten buried in the covers. I gave into temptation and opened the book instead. Just a little while, I thought.

* * *

With clean hair and a baggy jacket, I thought I looked almost okay. It was a good thing I'd taught this class many times before as I'd read the mystery novel right up until Victoria arrived with my lunch. I'd asked her to wash my hair, and she kindly obliged, though it was sort of a production.

A rolling plastic sink with a water tank below was lodged in another corner of the room. I scooted around until my head was at the edge of the bed on a plastic sheet Victoria had placed there. Then I hung my head further back and it rested on the neck support of the sink. In a remarkably short amount of time, Victoria had wet my hair, shampooed it, and then carefully used the spray apparatus to rinse it. A cap-shaped towel was slipped over my wet hair, and I was able to scoot back.

"Oh, thanks, Victoria," I said as she combed out my clean hair and then got out the hair dryer. "It feels so good to have clean hair."

"I know, I know," she burbled in her sweet way. "I hate a dirty scalp. Icky!"

Victoria said things like "icky," but I'd learned she was no creampuff. And Tom's brother Dave was smitten with her. His time with Doctors Without Borders seemed to have taken a lot out of him, at least according to Tom, and Victoria was helping him find more fun in life even as he went around the southside of Chicago opening clinics in his new job.

Victoria went back downstairs to do some more work on her wedding business, and I pulled my thoughts over to Religion in America.

I knew from my previous pregnancy that the swelling of the last months included increased fluid in the cranium and that made it harder to focus. A friend of mind had called this "milk on the brain," and it was accurate.

I had a printed list of the students next to my computer so I could remember their names if I blanked, and I reviewed it.

I had a few of the "need a humanities distribution" folks like Elaine Myers, pre-med, Joseph Crossan, lapsed Catholic who was a robotics engineering major, and that was a new area at the university, I'd learned from him, or Ravi Balakrishnan, an economics major, though he was dual majoring in philosophy. Ipswitch Featherstone, environmental biology major and Wiccan, was kind of a new presence for me, though when I'd taught a class in a prison last spring, one of the students had been a Wiccan. Then there were always those who were trying to come to terms with their conservative religious upbringing. This year I had Jae Hoon Lee, Korean, whose father was a pastor in Seoul, and Imelda Jackson, sociology major, already a deacon in her Missionary Baptist Church, but subtly exhibiting the push/pull of her intense belief and her commitment to social analysis. And there were those who were majoring and who planned on going to seminary or graduate school in religion like Alison Ackerman or Harrison Fisher, though those two were quite different from each other. Alison was United Church of Christ and a liberal through and through, while Fisher was of a Reformed Church background.

Well, today they were all going to get how religious opposition to the atomic age had initiated the interfaith work that we saw so much of today.

I turned on the computer, pulled up the bookcase background I used (I would let no student see me in bed!) and hit the icon to start the class.

"Welcome to Religion in America. Today we are going to examine how the current interfaith cooperation in this country was actually a product of religious opposition to the nuclear age."

Harrison's hand shot up.

"Yes, Harrison?"

I'd barely begun, and he was already tense.

"Do you mean all religions like Muslims too?"

"I believe you mean Islam, right Harrison? And yes, many Muslims do oppose atomic weapons."

He leaned forward like he was going to speak again and Ipswitch, who was sitting next to him, interjected in her melodious voice, a voice I suspected she practiced.

"Let go, Harrison, and permit the lecture to flow," she said.

He got even more red in the face.

It was going to be a long hour.

5

~

We can deny our experience, but our body remembers.

— **Jeanne McElvaney**, *Spirit Unbroken: Abby's Story*

"So, what now? You got a couple weeks more of this stayin' in bed and then the babies are born?" Alice Matthews said in a monotone, staring out my front bedroom window.

Since she'd arrived, she'd barely looked at me. It had only been a few days since we'd seen each other, but I'd swear she'd lost weight, and she was certainly tense. Her shoulder blades were pulled back so sharply they nearly crossed in the middle of her back.

What was up? It had taken me three days and five phone messages to get her here.

"Yes, that's what they tell me, Alice," I said as calmly as I could. I needed to find out what was wrong, because clearly something was. The problem was that absolutely the last thing Alice would ever accept was any expression of concern from me, or really, from anyone, at least from what I'd observed over the years.

No reply. More staring out the window.

"Come on over here and sit. It's hard for me to turn and look at you way over there," I said levelly.

And that was true. The only position that was remotely comfortable for me was propped up on pillows with my legs in what a yoga teacher would call butterfly position, knees slightly bent and feet touching. Twisting around to see someone who was nearly behind me was hard. Well, no. It was impossible. My middle did not twist.

"Yeah."

Alice turned and with robot stiff legs walked over to the chair next to the bed. She folded at the waist and barely touched her bottom to the chair. She was effectively crouching, ready to spring up.

Her face was definitely thinner, and there were new lines in her normally smooth, mocha-colored skin. I looked closely. She was sweating. Rivulets of sweat were running down her face along her hairline. Then I sniffed. She's smoking again, I thought. The smell of tobacco was faint, but it was definitely coming off her.

We'd known each other for several years, had each other's backs in life and death situations, and, I thought, were close friends. I decided to address the elephant in the room.

"What's up, Alice? You're tense, you're sweating, and you are not acting like yourself. Is it Jim, or Shawna? Come on. We've known each other too long for this. You know I'll get it out of you eventually." I had kept my tone light, but the more I spoke, the more she visibly drew in on herself.

"Nothin', okay, just nothin'. Don't push," she mumbled, then her voice rose. "Don't you dare push me!" She grabbed her hair with both hands and pulled on the normally dark, springy curls. They too had looked flat, almost crushed, when she'd come in. Now she kept pulling on her hair, hard. It had to be excruciating. And her eyes were half closed.

I scooted my butt along the bed and swung my legs over the side. I gently put my hands on her hands that were literally trying to tear her hair out of her scalp. I just let my hands lightly cover her hands, but I made no move to stop her.

She stopped. Her eyes opened, and she seemed to see me. She sat back. Then she really focused on me.

"You get yourself and those babies back into that bed, you hear?" she said, but in a raspier voice than I'd ever heard her use.

"Yes, Alice," I said quietly and did what she said.

"I can't talk about it, Kristin. I can't. I really just can't. You gotta stop asking. I can't," she said, the despair in her voice breaking my heart.

"Whatever it is, Alice, I'm here," I said.

"Yeah, yeah. Little Miss Fix It." But getting angry at me seemed to relax her a little and she sat back in the chair, her eyes closed.

Then she opened her eyes, their dark irises almost black, and looked beyond me to only something she could see.

"Listen, I gotta go. You take care of yourself, you hear?"

She grabbed her jacket and hat from where she'd left them on a chair by the door and ran out of the room.

What in the name of all that is holy was that? I thought. Whatever it was, it was darned serious.

I thought if there were something wrong with her daughter or her husband, she'd at least have acknowledged that. Alice didn't "share," so to speak. She was a very private person. But we did talk about our lives, our problems, some.

This was something, else, something deeply personal to her. To her? About her?

I knew enough about PTSD to know the signs, and Alice was exhibiting them, big time. She had seemed so anxious looking out the window from the back she could have been on a dangerous stake out. She had seemed hyper-alert. She had gotten angry at the slightest question, and her self-harming in pulling out her hair was truly alarming.

If not her home life, I guessed, then it had to be something on the job.

I opened my computer and looked up the campus paper. The big thing that had happened was the drowning death of that swim coach. I scanned back through the articles. They didn't say who'd found the body, but I knew Alice had been taking more night shifts since Jim's hours had been cut. Maybe she'd been the one to find the body.

I scanned further back to the day after what the paper called the "incident." The articles didn't say who'd found his body, but then they wouldn't, would they, if it were one of the campus police?

The babies took that moment to start high kicks in my abdomen like they were in a ballet class, or that's what it felt like, and I had to lean way back onto the pillows to get some relief.

I stared at the ceiling, searching for possible connections, starting with swimming.

About two years ago, I had wondered whether I should enroll the boys not only in the swim classes at our "Y," but also sign them up for the team as well. I had decided to discuss it with Alice.

"Are you having Shawna take swim lessons? Is she on a team as well?" I'd asked her. She and Jim lived in the same southside town where she'd grown up, and they had a good, public swim facility. It was not like the "whites only" communities where African Americans were kept off swim teams. Her town's teams were so good they competed city-wide, and I'd seen photos in the paper of the diverse team members.

"No and no," she'd said flatly.

"Oh," I'd said. "I swam as a kid and even into my teens. Did you?"

"Yes."

It had been like pulling teeth.

"So, why isn't she even learning to swim?"

"Drop it, okay?" Alice had said. And I knew that tone. It meant "drop it."

There had been something in her tone, something to do with the swimming that had stuck with me as very odd.

Maybe if Alice had been the one to find the body, it had triggered bad memories for her about swimming. I did not like that hair pulling. Not at all. Whatever it was, it was very alarming.

Well, if she wouldn't talk to me, I'd call her partner, Mel Billman. Both of us knew her well enough that we would definitely keep such a conversation to ourselves.

6

~

There is no timestamp on trauma. There isn't a formula that you can insert yourself into to get from horror to healed. Be patient. Take up space. Let your journey be the balm.

— Dawn Serra

I WOKE WITH A start from a nap. I had been dreaming about Alice drowning. Well, that fit. I sat up a little straighter in the bed and tried to breathe normally.

It was so annoying how tired I was getting these days. We had a visiting nurse, a nice Polish lady, Mrs. Janowski, who came by after lunch and helped me with using the portable toilet. I was absolutely not going to let anyone else but Tom do that, and even his help made me uncomfortable. She also changed the sheets and took my vital signs.

Then, each day, she bundled the sheets up and took them down the hall to where the washer and dryer were located, blessedly on the second floor. I'd watched her walk down the hall and could hear the work on the second-floor bedrooms clearly when the door to our bedroom was open. I knew the plumbing had been finished for those baths, along with the kitchen plumbing. There was faint whining, I thought from a tile saw in the backyard, and then upstairs the scrape, scape, scrape of the sand-based adhesive used to set tile being troweled on. Good. We seemed to still by on schedule.

Mrs. Janowski came back, asked if I needed anything else. I'd said no, and that was the last I had remembered.

I scooted up a little more against the pillows. What was I planning to do this afternoon? There was something and it felt urgent. The "milk on the brain" was getting worse. I sat for a few minutes trying to remember.

I need to start writing things down, I grumbled to myself. I needed to get the pad and pen that I had and looked around. I saw that Mrs. Janowski had placed them on the table near the bed with my computer and cell phone. But she'd clearly moved the table back to get at the sheets. Sigh. I scooted to the edge of the bed and reached out to bring everything back on to the bed. I fumbled, trying to get them all in one reach, and the pad hit the floor. No bending down for that, I thought, frustrated all over again.

Anyway, I thought as I leaned back against the pillows again, I got the cell and the computer.

Cell. That triggered my swollen brain.

Call Mel Billman.

I had his cell phone number in my phone and pressed "call." It went quickly to voicemail, so I left a message.

"Mel, this is Kristin Ginelli. It's about Alice. Call me, would you?"

That would do it, I thought. Mel and Alice were often partnered, and they were certainly friends.

Mel, over the years I'd known him, was steady as a rock. He was broad-shouldered and tall, a little over my 6 foot. He was a man of few words, but he stepped up. I knew him to be smart and courageous, having once tracked murderers through a tunnel under the university quad and another time having identified white supremacists who were using online gaming to plan attacks on campus. He'd even put himself between those same white supremacists and our Muslim faculty member, Aduba Abubakar, last year's hire in Philosophy and Religion. Aduba had given a talk despite there being threats against him. I'd lent him my bullet-proof vest, but that didn't guarantee his safety.

My phone rang. Mel.

"Kristin, what's up?" Mel began.

How to start.

"Well, Mel, I'm a little concerned about Alice."

"Yeah, well, you and me both," Mel said, his voice deepening with concern. "She's on a temporary leave."

"Why?" I asked, my stomach giving a heave.

"You know what, where are you? I think we should talk about this in person."

Oh, I hated to have to tell Mel I was so incapacitated. No choice, though. I was not going to have him come here and see me like this.

"Mel, I'm having to rest in bed because of the twins. Can we just talk on the phone?"

"Sure, sure. I get it. Sorry. Here, just let me walk a little where I won't be overheard. So, Alice tells me you're expecting girls. When are they due, again?"

"Two weeks, Mel, though every day feels like a month."

He chuckled.

"Yeah, yeah. When Makena was expecting, she said the same. And the amount of Butter Pecan ice cream that woman put away made me think Malia would be made largely of cream, butter, and pecans."

Malia, his daughter, was named for his grandmother whom I had learned from Alice lived on the Navajo nation in Arizona.

I chuckled at the image of a baby made of cream and nuts. Mel's voice changed, and he interrupted that picture.

"So," Mel said, "I think this is private enough. Listen, and well, you know, and this is strictly between us, there was that swim coach who was found drowned?"

"Yes, I've read about it at least," I said.

"Well, it's been determined that Alice was the one who found the body in the pool, and she did not call it in."

"Oh, man, Mel, that's not good."

"You're telling me. You know, Captain Gutierrez checked the duty roster yesterday morning and saw she had been on. He demanded she come in and turn in her body camera. It's not on for video all the time, but it does track where we are by GPS. He saw she'd entered the pool area and immediately left again, and he really reamed her out. Suspended her."

"Oh, God, Mel. That's awful. Is she a suspect, is that what you're telling me?"

"Yeah, I think so." His voice sounded like he was at the bottom of a well, and I thought he must be cupping his hand over his phone.

"She was just here at my house, and I tell you Mel, and this is between us, her behavior was disturbing. She was exhibiting extreme symptoms of stress."

"I tried to talk with her, Kristin, after she'd seen Gutierrez," Mel said. "She shut me out cold. Really unusual. I wanted to know why she'd fled the scene. Nothing. She just looked through me."

I had no trouble believing that.

"You know, Mel. I think there's something about pools and swimming that scare Alice. Do you know if she maybe had a near drowning experience or something like that? Maybe seeing a drowning victim set her off."

"I don't know, but the rumor mill is working overtime, Kristin. She's been told to make herself available for an interview with the Chicago detective leading the investigation."

Oh, God. Chicago detectives. I had been one for a short time and the sexual harassment, casual violence and corruption had been horrific. Then my husband Marco, also a detective, had been murdered in the line of duty. I'd suspected a really terrible detective of having had a hand in it, but that had turned out not to be true. That guy had been fired though, for other reasons.

"Who's the detective?" I asked, dreading the answer.

"Jake Booth. White guy, pretty senior. He'd been with the Chicago department twenty years ago or so, was recruited up to Wisconsin, now he's back. Squeaky clean rep. They needed somebody after all that murder and corruption came out last year."

Yes, murder and corruption that Mel, Alice and I had helped to expose.

Twenty years ago, I thought. I wondered if Marco's father had known him, even if briefly. I contemplated calling Vince Ginelli and asking but mentally put that off. Vince had had a stroke this past winter, and he was still recuperating at home in Wisconsin.

"Listen, Mel, do you know if Alice has a lawyer?"

"No idea. Really, when I saw her, she looked like a ghost, though I shouldn't say that or my *ke'eehe*, my grandmother, will get on me. But get this, I did just hear that the dead swim coach had coached in Alice's hometown fifteen to twenty years ago, right when Alice would have been a teen."

Not good. Not good at all.

"So, she could have known him, that's what you're saying the rumor mill is churning out?"

"Right. She's gotta be a suspect, Kristin," Mel said, his deep voice vibrating with concern.

"Mel, keep me posted, will you? I'll try to talk to Alice."

"Good luck with that," he said. "But don't stress yourself out too much with the babies and all."

"No, I won't," I lied.

Maybe I was stuck here in this bed, but I could get Alice a good lawyer.

I picked up the phone and called my friend and attorney supreme, Anna Feldman.

7

~

Trauma survivors may present to police with flat or restricted affect, emotional numbing, and disjointed recollections.

—*Sage Journals*, **May 12, 2019**

Just as I reached out for my cell phone, it rang. I checked the display. It was Anna.

"Hi, Anna. Good timing. I was just about to call you," I said.

"Well, I'm two blocks from your house, and I can be there in minutes. I had a deposition at the university, and it finished early," Anna said in her melodious voice. "I have a baby shower present for you."

Oh no. I didn't want Anna, who dressed so elegantly and who was always so beautifully turned out, to see me this way, a blob in a tent dress in the middle of a messy bed.

"Anna, really," I said hurriedly. "Not necessary. We have every baby thing a person can imagine and in duplicate. Why don't we just talk on the phone?" I said in a rush.

"Too late. I'm here."

I heard a car pull up outside. Anna didn't drive. She used a limo service and claimed it was cheaper than having a car in the city and having to pay to park it. She'd be at the door in seconds.

"Anna, the code is star 81597 pound," I said resignedly. We'd had a keypad lock installed with all these people coming and going. No need for keys.

"Oh, and Anna, Molly is loose in the house," I said into the phone, but realized I was speaking to dead air. I reached over for my hairbrush on the end table and gave my bed hair a few, rapid strokes. Best I could do, I sighed.

I heard the front door open and the sound of dog claws on the parquet wood floors.

"Ah. The dog," I heard Anna say. "No, dog. Down."

I heard a thunk. Molly's paws hitting the floor. Molly obeying Anna. Prosecutors and even judges obeyed Anna when she talked to them in that tone of voice, so I was not surprised a Golden Retriever would.

"I'm up here," I called.

"I'm coming," Anna said. I could hear what were likely her Louboutin heels clicking on the stair treads.

The next minute, she appeared in the bedroom doorway. She deftly entered the room and shut the door firmly with Molly outside.

She looked great as usual. I'd never seen what looked like a Versace long suit jacket and straight leg pants outfit that she had on, though I was not surprised. She owned so many beautiful clothes and wielded them like a medieval knight would use a shield and a lance, both to defend and to disarm.

Anna went to Hong Kong twice a year to get her clothes custom made. "I have a black belt in shopping," she'd once told me, and I believed it.

Gold was the theme for the jewelry today. She used fabulous jewelry like Madeleine Albright had used her dramatic pins, to deliberately distract opponents while she disposed of them.

I wanted to put the bed cover over my head I felt like such a frump, but instead I smiled and said I was so glad to see her.

"Well, you're having a time of it, aren't you?" she said, bringing a large, square box with silver and pink wrapping from behind her back and handing it to me.

"Thank you, Anna," I said, feeling the weight of it.

She settled into the visitor's chair.

"Well, open it!" she exclaimed, clearly anticipating my reaction to the gift.

Anna did not have children, so I prepared myself to praise whatever she had brought.

I pulled the exquisite pink bow off and carefully slid the silver and pink paper off the box.

Then I squealed with joy. I couldn't help it.

"William Curley Venezuelan Gold Chocolate Truffles!"

Anna smiled.

"Go ahead. Open it and have one. Or more than one," she said, clearly enjoying my response.

"Oh, Anna. I will." I lifted the lid. There were two tiers of the award-winning chocolate. Oh my. I dithered over the selection, finally selecting a "Chocolate Supreme."

I popped it in my mouth, and it filled me with such pleasure I thought I might be having an orgasm.

"Wan' on'?" I mumbled, my mouth full of the dense confection.

Anna laughed.

"No, no. How could I take away even one moment of the happiness you'll experience with these," she said, leaning back and smiling.

"Jus' one more," I said, pulling another one from its little gold foil nest and chomping it before I'd totally finished the first one.

I munched contentedly and contemplated my good friend sitting there enjoying giving me pleasure. A friendship to treasure, I thought.

All too soon, though, the second truffle was gone. I picked up my Tommy Tippy cup and took a drink of water.

I thought for a minute and then began.

"So, Anna, here's what's happening."

She drew out her phone from her bag and used a stylus to take notes.

I went through as much as I knew, quoting Mel Billman and noting there was proof Alice had entered the pool area and left again immediately.

"How immediately?" Anna asked, stylus poised over the screen.

"I don't know, but I imagine Mel could find out."

She was right. It was key point. If it were seconds, even a minute or so, Alice could be in the clear. Longer than that, she'd have had time to commit a murder.

I went on describing Alice's behavior, listing the PTSD characteristics I'd observed myself.

"And apparently, according to her colleague on the campus police force, she could have known him from his time as the swim coach of a team in the suburbs. The timing and location are right. I've wondered about possible abuse from that time like we've been reading about happened on other swim teams such as the ones in California."

"Possible," Anna said, tapping her stylus on the screen. "Is she seeing a therapist? Could be vital to document the PTSD."

"I don't know, but I doubt it, frankly. I know someone good I can recommend to her, but honestly, Anna, the woman is so stubborn. She'll say no a million times before she says yes to that."

"Not that unusual in survivors," Anna commented while she wrote. She looked up. "They have carefully constructed walls around a traumatic event and anything that threatens to breach those walls will be met with a strong, defensive backlash."

"Well, speaking of defense," I said, "she doesn't have a lawyer and she really can't afford one, Anna. She won't accept my help. I was wondering if you knew someone who could take this on pro bono."

"Yes, let me see what I can come up with. I know a senior litigation associate who came out of the Illinois State's Attorney's office before he went into our firm who might take this on pro bono. I'll have to persuade my partners to permit that, but, as I think about it, one of the our managing partners had a daughter who was abused by a teacher. That is totally confidential, but he'd be supportive of the firm having someone take this on. I'll check when I get back to the office and probably get back to you tomorrow in the morning."

"These abusers are everywhere, Anna," I said, thinking of Anna's partner's daughter and her parents. Then I thought about my own kids both outside and inside my womb. Gave me a chill.

"Okay, then," Anna said, putting her phone and stylus away and texting her car service.

"Two weeks more in bed and then the birth?"

"Yes," I said. "The chocolates are already helping make that more manageable," I said and smiled up at her as she got up.

"You're right that your friend needs representation, and see if you can get her to see that therapist," she said, snapping her bag closed.

"I will," I said, inhaling her Chanel Coco perfume one last time. She never used too much. It was just like a pleasant cloud around her. I had a stab of worry about what this bedroom must smell like to her. There were many smells that I bet were lingering in the air.

Anna waved good-bye as she opened the door, and Molly shot into the room. She'd plainly been sitting by the door.

"Open or closed?" Anna asked.

"Oh, leave it open, please. The boys will be home shortly."

"Alright. Bye again," she said and clicked back down the stairs.

Molly's nose was zeroing in on the truffles.

"None of that for you, Molly girl," I said. "These could kill you."

I had a plastic bag of dog treats attached to the bedframe on my side of the bed, and I reached back for a substantial chew for her.

When she settled down with it, I took another of the chocolate truffles out of the box and savored it.

Where am I going to hide these? I wondered. I could keep them under the covers until Tom came home, and he could hide them more thoroughly. Oh, but then how will I get at them during the day? I worried.

My end table was quite large, with three drawers. I rolled over and opened the top drawer. Lot of useless junk.

I pulled the junk out and deposited most of it in the trash can by my side of the bed. The rest, like emery boards, nail polish, and assorted combs I put on the top of the end table. That surface was getting pretty crowded I noticed.

Then I went to slip the truffle box into the newly empty drawer. Wait, I thought. Just one more. I took one out and was going to save it for a little while, but I heard the door open, and two voices called "Mom!"

"Hi!" I called, and then I guiltily crammed the whole truffle in my mouth.

* * *

I heard about their day in school, and I examined two math papers, both with "100%" written in red across the top.

"Snack!" Carol had called from downstairs, and the boys thundered down. I wonder what they weigh these days, I thought idly.

Then Mrs. Janowski arrived. She shut the door and went about letting me complete my toilet time. She brought over the portable sink, and I washed my face. I didn't even use the little mirror I had on the end table. What does it matter? I thought.

* * *

The boys were down the hall in their bedroom doing their homework before dinner. I could hear occasional grunts or snorts as they settled at their desks (or more likely on their beds since I couldn't go check.)

Well, I thought, I could give Rev. Dr. Pearson Hill a call. She was a former police chaplain, which is how I had met her, who had been working on a Ph.D. in psychology. She had finished with that a couple of years ago and gone into private practice, specializing in trauma in women, particularly African American women. She'd be a perfect therapist for Alice if only I could get her to go.

I called, and it went to voicemail.

I left a message asking her to call me as it was about a potential client who had very urgent issues. I repeated my cell phone number even though I knew she had it.

I was getting tired, and my back hurt a little. I shifted around, trying to get comfortable, but the small ache wouldn't go away.

Then Tom appeared in the doorway carrying a tray. Giles was just behind him with a second one.

We tried hard to still have family meals, and the TV tables were set up with folding chairs and our meal spread out, mine on my bed tray. Tom called the boys.

They raced down the hall, Molly close behind.

"Hey Mom! Hey Pop!" they chorused. "We're going to try out for the swim team this winter at school."

"That's great, boys," Tom said. "Now sit down and eat. Remember, no food for Molly from your plates."

Oh, yeah, great, I thought.

I certainly would run a criminal background check on their school swim coach.

8

Women's bodies have near-perfect knowledge of childbirth; it's when their brains get involved that things can go wrong.

-Peggy Vincent

Tom had gotten up quite early again this morning, clearly intent on getting out of the house quickly. I felt like I was on a timer while I used the portable toilet.

I was still feeling achy in my lower back, but that was normal, right? I was just sitting around all the time looking like Ninhursag, the hugely pregnant Sumerian Mother Goddess with a big belly and pendulous breasts. Since Ninhursag had given birth to both gods and humans, she probably had felt like I did this morning a lot of the time.

I was bored. The boys weren't up yet and here I was gestating all by myself.

Oh, I could eat a chocolate truffle. I reached into the drawer and snagged one. Delicious. Just one, I told myself.

Finally, as the digital clock turned to 7 am, the cell phone rang. Anna. Oh, good. Anna started work just after dawn, it seemed.

"Yes, Anna," I said.

"Yes is correct," she said briskly. "I had a chance to talk to that managing partner last night, and he approved asking Benjamin Acosta, a former Illinois Assistant States Attorney who has joined the firm, to take on Alice

Matthews' case pro bono. We just had a coffee in the office, and he's quite interested in helping out. He's a good man, Kristin, and he's a good lawyer."

She then started to dictate his contact information.

"Wait, wait, I need to get a pad and pen," I said looking over at the increasingly crowded top of the end table.

"No, don't stir yourself. I'll just text you his details."

I heard a text tone.

"Thank you so much, Anna," I said warmly, "and thanks again for the chocolate."

"You're welcome. Call me when the girls are born, or," she chuckled, "shortly thereafter," and she ended the call.

"Did you say 'chocolate,'?" Mike asked, coming in with Molly. Sam was behind him, dragging his beloved blanket. We never said anything about Sam's blanket. In our house, if you needed a blanket, you got a blanket.

"Mike, it's not nice to listen in on other people's calls," I said, dodging the issue.

"Where's Pop?" Sam asked.

"Already gone. Early case."

Sam yawned.

"When I'm a doctor, I'll start later," he said, crawling up on to the bed and curling up.

This was the first I'd heard Sam say he wanted to be a doctor. I smiled down at his bedhead. If he did become a doctor, he'd find out about the hours on his own.

It was finally quiet again. Carol had gathered up the boys with a minimum of fuss and left with them to walk to their school and her job.

The cell phone rang again, and "Shannon Pearson Hill" displayed on the screen. My therapist friend.

Oh, good. It wasn't even 9 am and my plans for the day were about to finish up.

"Hello, Shannon," I said, grateful to talk to yet another adult.

"Hello yourself, and how is the human hatchery feeling today?" she asked, both humor and concern in her voice.

"Just about like that, Shannon. And if Tom pats my stomach again instead of kissing me, he's going to get a giant wake-up call about how I'm still the woman he married, not a carrying case for his babies!"

Wow. I realized I'd been hauling that feeling around for a while. Felt good to say it to a trustworthy person.

"Well, I'll stop by, maybe next week, and give you an ear for those feelings," she said.

"Thanks. I'd like that. It's my colleague Alice Matthews I'm calling about, though."

I went through a brief synopsis of what I'd observed in Alice. I kept quiet about the lawyer and the cops. If Alice did see her, she could share that if she chose.

"Sure, sure. I'd love to see her. Give her this private cell number, would you? That way we can shorten the process of getting her in to see me. Sounds like issues could be coming to a head," she said and started to state some numbers.

Oh, I should have had the boys bring my pad and pen over. Where was my head?

"Could you just text that to me?" I asked.

"Of course. Take care now. You're almost at the finish line."

"Oh, I keep telling myself that, Shannon, but I'm feeling so tired of it all."

"Totally natural. You know, call that private cell number if you need to vent before I get there next week," she said.

"Thanks," I said. "I am grateful, truly." And we hung up.

* * *

Eight cell phone calls to Alice later, I still hadn't reached her. Mrs. Janowski and come and gone. At least now I had a pen and paper, and I transferred all the names and contact information, both the lawyer and the therapist, to two pieces of paper to give Alice.

Giles had brought me a sandwich, but I really had no appetite.

I decided to switch to texting.

"Alice, I can keep this up all day. I have nothing else to do. Call me."

Just then I heard the front door open. Probably Victoria. Then I heard Alice's voice.

"Yeah, yeah, dog. It's me. No need to sniff me again."

"Alice?" I called.

"You bugging the hell out of somebody else? Yeah. Who else would it be?"

I was glad to hear that grumpy voice. It was music to my ears compared to the monotone and then the hair pulling of her last visit.

"Come on up."

"Yeah, yeah. And dog, you quit that," she said as she came up the stairs.

Like Anna, when she got to our bedroom, Alice closed the door to shut Molly out. I could hear all 75 pounds of Molly hit the floor in a lump outside in the hall.

"So?" she said, glaring at me.

"Hi, Alice. Good to see you too. I'm feeling tired and achy in my back, but other than that I'm fine," I said, trying to get back to our usual banter.

"Always so cute," she said wearily. She came over and nearly collapsed into the chair by the bed.

I looked closely at her. Her hair was unwashed; it almost looked like it hadn't been combed for days. She wasn't wearing her uniform so obviously she was still suspended. She had on a print cotton shirt, jeans, and a light tan cotton jacket. All were wrinkled. They looked like they had just been pulled out of a dirty clothes hamper. And yes, I could really smell the cigarette smoke coming off her.

She wasn't hovering over the chair this time. She looked like she was trying to merge with the cushions. But I couldn't count on her staying around, so I thought I'd better jump in.

I tore the two sheets of paper from my pad and reached them out toward her. She hesitated a minute and then took them.

"The first name and contact information is for a pro bono lawyer Anna's firm has arranged. His name is Benjamin Acosta, and he's a former Illinois Assistant States Attorney."

She started to protest, and I held up my hand.

"Just wait," I said firmly. "Mel has filled me in, and you are an idiot if you are talking to the Chicago police without a lawyer present. Do I need to remind you that you have a daughter, a husband, and a mother who all need you? You need to stay out of jail."

Her face went blank.

I couldn't let it stop me.

"The other name and contact information is for a therapist, Rev. Dr. Shannon Pearson Hill. She's a good friend of mine, a former Chicago police department chaplain, and she specializes in PTSD."

Still blank. No reaction.

I stopped. I felt a huge cramp, and the bed flooded with water.

"Alice," I said, moaning and rolling slightly over to my side.

"Oh, hell. You're in labor," Alice said sharply, and she pulled out her cell phone.

"What's Tom's cell number?" she asked.

"I . . . I can't think," I said as another pain hit me.

Alice picked up my phone, put it in front of my face so it would open with my facial recognition and then she took it back and thumbed the screen, I guessed to scroll to contacts.

"Goin' to voicemail. Damn," she said. "Tom Grayson, this is Alice Matthews. Your wife is going into labor, and I'm calling an ambulance. My cell phone is 773-245-8841."

She immediately punched in three numbers. Must be 911, I thought woozily, and she gave my address and a bunch of information I couldn't really follow now.

"They'll be here in five," she said, leaning over to help me sit up.

I groaned.

"You got any of those paper bed pads around? I could sop up some of this water," she said.

She opened the first drawer of the end table.

"Chocolate?" she exclaimed. "You eatin' a bunch of chocolate? Don't you know that brings on labor, you idiot?" Now she really sounded like herself.

"That's, that's an old wives' tale, Alice," I said, summoning the energy to defend my chocolate.

"Yeah, right. You eat chocolate and go into early labor, and I'm telling tales? Not damn likely." Alice was really getting mad. I was so glad to see it. *Post hoc, ergo propter hoc*, I thought. The Latin phrase we in philosophy rejected because it meant just because something followed something else, it was caused by it. But I wasn't out of it enough to quote Latin as a defense of my chocolate to Alice.

Then a labor pain hit me, and I groaned again.

Breathe, I thought.

I heard Molly scratch at the door.

Molly. The kids. My class.

"Alice," I breathed between what were now clearly contractions, "call Carol Diop, contact's in the phone. Tell her. Tell her."

"Okay. Right." She did that and blessedly reached Carol who only worked two blocks away at her social worker job.

"She'll come, take over," Alice said.

We both looked up hearing the ambulance pull up and the siren cut off.

"I'll go down and let them in," Alice said.

"Put the dog in the library," I breathed.

"Yeah, yeah."

I had another contraction.

I should be timing these, I thought woozily.

Then the ambulance guys came in and asked if I could walk.

"I don't know," I said.

They brought a sling contraption and carried me out to the ambulance.

"I'll meet you in the Emergency Room," Alice called. "I have your purse."

The last I saw of Alice she was heading for her car. The ambulance blared its way to the hospital that was mercifully only two blocks past the university campus. The doors of the ambulance were opened, and I saw a gurney come out of the doors of the ER. Tom was hurrying beside it.

I wanted to say hi but instead I groaned again.

Two hours later Olivia and Natalie Ginelli Grayson were born. They would spend the night in the neonatal unit for preemies as a precaution, but since they were each 6 pounds, they seemed quite healthy.

Alice came by the recovery room and handed me my purse.

"You okay?" she asked, but her blank face was back in place.

"You may have saved the girls' lives. You may have saved my life," I said seriously. "Thank you."

She nodded and turned to go.

"Now save your own life. Call those numbers," I said to her back.

She shrugged her shoulders and left.

I dug out my cell phone from my purse and called my colleague, Nia Turner.

We had arranged she'd take the class for me if the babies came early.

"Nia?" I said when I heard her voice.

"Yes, what's up?"

"The babies just made an appearance," I said, fatigue creeping into my voice.

"Oh, wonderful. And don't worry about a thing. I'm on it." I expressed my thanks, and she rung off.

Then I saw Tom in the doorway. I was so glad he'd been able to be in the delivery room with me. He hurried over to the bedside.

"Oh, Kristin. You. Our girls." I saw tears in his eyes. "I love you all so much."

He bent over me, and there was no more stomach patting. We stayed like that for a while. Then Tom stood up.

"I'll be by later, accompany you to your room," he said.

"Good," I sighed. I saw him leave and started to drift off.

Then my eyes snapped wide open.

Oh my God! I thought. The nanny doesn't start for another week.

9

The conflict between the will to deny horrible events and the will to proclaim them aloud is the central dialectic of psychological trauma.

— **Judith Lewis Herman**, *Trauma and Recovery*

Alice drove slowly along in the bumper-to-bumper traffic, but she scarcely saw the road. What she saw on the windshield was her daughter Shawna's face framed by dozens of braids with little, dangling bows.

Damn Kristin. Damn her for bringing up Shawna and the threat of leaving her and going to jail. Jim would deal, but not Shawna. And miss all that growing? And Mama was getting' older, less energy. No, no. Can't take my child away from me.

She'd stood at the window of the neonatal unit in the hospital staring at Kristin's little girls. Tiny little bundles so tightly wrapped they looked like pink sausages. Safe and secure.

She shivered with fear.

That detective, that Booth, he'd been so smooth, tryin' to be understanding, "Just tell me what happened. We can figure it out."

Wants to see me in two days downtown. Lettin' me sweat, but oh so nice on the phone.

"Just come by, we'll go over it again. You're helping so much."

Oh yeah, right. A white detective on my side, his grey hair and glasses around a fake, kind face. Oh no. Just fittin' me up to do the time. That's what they did, white cops. They pushed you and pulled you and wore you out and they hoped you'd make one tiny mistake. Not even make a mistake. They'd lie. They were such liars. Make stuff up. Then, they'd send you to a hole of a prison like Joliet used to be. So bad they closed it. How bad does a prison have to be to get closed for being bad?

No. Not going to prison. Not happening.

And no work. No paycheck. And there was a mortgage payment coming up.

Her insides churned with fear.

Damn Kristin for being right. Never tell her that though, she'd just push more.

A horn honked behind her. She had stopped the car.

She sped up slightly.

Can't afford an accident. They'd had to let the car insurance lapse.

When I get off this stupid highway, I'll call that lawyer Kristin found. Acosta.

But I'll be damned if I call some shrink doctor. No way. I been doin' fine. Just forget about it and get those racist cops off my back.

She took her suburban exit and pulled over into a Denny's parking lot.

She pulled out the paper Kristin had given her with the lawyer's name and number. She dialed, thought about the message she'd leave.

"Ben Acosta," a man's voice said.

She felt like she'd stuck her finger in a light socket. He'd answered. Himself.

"Oh, oh. Mr. Acosta. My name is Alice Matthews."

"Excellent, Ms. Matthews. I've been expecting your call."

Oh Jesus, Alice thought, as he told her where to meet him the next day.

10

~

You don't scare me. I'm the mother of two sets of twins.

—**Dr. Kristin Ginelli**

Tom and I headed down to the neonatal unit to see the girls. I also wanted to start them at the breast even though they would probably not take to it yet. But it would help with my milk coming in.

The pediatrician wanted to keep them in the NICU for another 24 to 48 hours. Natalie, named for the indomitable mother of my first husband, Marco, had been born first and Olivia, named for Tom's gentle, wheelchair bound mother, had been born 35 minutes later. They were living up to their names. Natalie was the more active; Olivia was quieter. Both needed to stay in their incubators a while longer to monitor their lungs, but we could spend time with them, cuddle them against our skin.

I heard Tom's sharp intake of breath as we rounded the corner and saw through the big window that his daughter Kelly from his first marriage was in one of the rocking chairs they kept in the unit, her t-shirt rucked up and Natalie pressed against her abdomen. He stopped, clearly stunned by seeing his daughter holding his other daughter. Or, more likely, his older daughter looking like a young mother.

We got our masks and went in.

"Hi, Kelly," I said, walking over to her and gently stroking Natalie's back.

"Hi Mom, hi Dad," she said softly. "Natalie was screaming her head off when I got here for a visit, so I showed them my I.D. and they let me come in and pick her up. She quieted right down."

She looked down proudly at the tiny head covered with a jaunty, too-large cap with some fuzz sticking out of the bottom.

Clearly Natalie's lungs were functioning well.

I went over to Olivia's incubator and picked her up. She was sound asleep. I carried her over to another rocker and sat down. I unbuttoned my pajama top and held her to my breast. She didn't open her eyes, but her tiny lips made sucking motions. I carefully placed my nipple between them, and I felt the familiar tug deep inside. My womb was contracting with the nipple stimulation. Good. The milk should come in soon. I'd had plenty of milk for both boys when they were born. I hoped that would be true for the older me.

I glanced up and saw Tom had taken Kelly's place in the rocker and had Natalie pressed against his bare chest. Kelly was sitting on a stool next to him, whispering something. I felt a stronger contraction inside and a drop of milk wet Olivia's lips. Her sucking motions increased slightly.

Kelly kissed her dad on the top of his head and whispered "Gotta go" to me.

"Thanks for helping," I whispered back.

"I think Carol plans to bring the boys this afternoon," she said softly. "If I can work it out, I'll come back with them."

"That's great," I breathed and watched her leave.

After a while, I whispered, "Let's switch" to Tom. He blinked for a second. He'd been in baby land, apparently. Easy to do.

I took Natalie. She was waking up some and clearly gearing herself up to yell again.

I touched her tiny lips with my finger and stimulated the sucking motion. She opened her eyes, and I didn't think I was imagining it, glared at me.

I placed her at my other breast, and she rubbed her face against it, clearly still mad. I gently moved her off the nipple and then back on. This time she did make the tiny, sucking movements, and my nipple responded with another drop of milk.

I might ask for a pumping machine, I thought, as my body remembered nursing, and I felt some milk let down.

Glancing over at Tom, I saw that he and Olivia were nearly sound asleep. She was tucked securely inside his shirt, so I didn't worry.

After about an hour with the girls, we went back to my room. I was tired out, but it felt so good to walk.

Our plan was for me to stay in the hospital while the girls were in the NICU. I was still bleeding quite a bit and my obstetrician, Dr. Eleanor Wiley, thought it prudent to monitor the risk of hemorrhage. Not that unusual with twins, though she thought my risk was low.

Back in the room, Tom helped me into bed. The room smelled almost uncomfortably floral as I'd had many bouquets delivered from friends and colleagues. I was going to keep the roses from my boss and friend, Adelaide Winters, but I'd asked the nurses if they'd donate the rest to the nursing home next door. I guessed no one had come to collect them yet.

Tom left, intending to pass his patients off to his colleagues. The early delivery had messed with his schedule too.

I wanted to doze off, but I thought I should call Carol and figure out when she was bringing the boys.

"I'll just walk them over after I pick them up at school," she said in her quiet, New England accented voice. "I'll let them run some on the way, drain off some of that energy."

"Good idea," I said.

Then I dialed Alejandro, the contractor.

"Felicidades, Mrs. G," he said. "We all happy for you and las niñas."

"Muchas gracias," I said, nearly exhausting my supply of Spanish.

Then I offered him a significant additional payment to get the nanny's room done by the end of this week.

"I can do it. I can pull men from another job. Today, we paint so no smell in a few days. Will work. You no worry," and he hung up.

Now, to see if the nanny could start early.

"Good morning, Mrs. Brown here," she answered briskly.

"Hello, Mrs. Brown," I said. "This is Kristin Ginelli. My twins were born early. Yesterday in fact. I was wondering if you could start earlier."

"I cannot leave the family I am with this week, but I could come a week from today. I had planned to take a short break, but I can accommodate you," she said in what I was coming to recognize as her "no nonsense" voice.

Good as I was going to get.

"Thank you," I said. "I will expect you then. Your room should be ready."

"Yes, it needs to be," Mrs. Brown said shortly. "Good-bye."

It was a little like talking to Nanny McPhee, the governess adapted for the movies from Christianna Brand's Nurse Matilda books. The boys loved the books and the movies. Though, I thought as my eyes closed, maybe they won't like that kind of discipline in real life.

* * *

"They're kinda small," Mike said critically, peering through the NICU window where Tom and Kelly held the girls up for Sam and Mike to see.

"Can they eat and stuff?" Sam wanted to know. "Cause, you know, they gotta grow before they can play."

"Yes," I said, an arm around each boy as we examined their new sisters. "They can have milk now, and pretty soon they'll be eating soft food. You guys can help feed them that. Even some milk when I push it out of my breasts and put it in a bottle."

Two shocked faces turned to me.

"That's gross," Sam said finally. Mike looked directly at my breasts like he feared milk would start to shoot out of them.

"Now, come on. You know that's where breast milk comes from. Breasts of Moms. You both drank breast milk and remember Molly thinking she was going to have puppies and her nipples swelled up?"

"Can we talk about something else?" Mike asked, turning back to the window.

Sam did the same. At almost 11, they were adjusting to the facts of reproduction and, so far, thinking that was "totally gross."

"So, which one is Natalie, and which one is Olivia?" Mike said, deftly changing the conversation.

"Pop is holding Olivia and Kelly is holding Natalie," I said as they gazed intently at the little faces.

"How come Kelly gets to go in there?" Mike asked suddenly.

"She's over 18 and an adult," I said, sensing a little sibling rivalry.

Sam laughed. "Yeah, right, Kelly's an adult."

"Could I go in and hold them each a little?" Carol asked softly. She had been standing behind us, and I had honestly forgotten she was there. Milk still on the brain.

"Of course, Carol. Just take a gown and mask from the cart by the door and put them on. It would be lovely if you could hold them some," I said.

Carol went in and shortly came up and took Natalie from Kelly. Natalie immediately started to yell. Carol looked alarmed, but Kelly helped her adjust how she was holding Natalie and then demonstrated the gentle back rubbing that worked so well with babies.

Fairly quickly Natalie calmed down. Carol's face was a study in contentment.

She's thinking about her own future babies, I thought. Then I thought, just let Giles graduate.

Finally, after Carol had held Olivia too, the babies were put back in their incubators, and she started to walk the boys down the hall toward the exit.

"Stop for ice cream on the way," I called to their retreating backs.

Both Sam and Mike punched the air to acknowledge they'd heard.

Despite my earlier nap, I was tired again and needed some rest. Tom walked me back to the room, and I lay down again. In about a minute I was out like a light.

* * *

It was late afternoon, and I was sitting up in bed using the double breast milk pump that had been delivered. The thing about using electric milk pumps is it is a little boring. It is hard to read a book or look at a screen because the pump jiggles your torso some and the page jumps around.

Books on tape were better or making calls.

Mel. I should check in with Mel, I thought, and dialed him.

"Hey Kristin. I hear congratulations are in order," Mel said when he picked up.

"Thanks, Mel. Yes. Two weeks early, but they seem to be doing well."

"That's great. Though two, Kristin. We just about went under with just one, though you've had twins before."

"Yeah, and 'going under' may describe it well, Mel. I'm still in the hospital. The twins need about another two days in incubators.

"Listen, I actually called to find out what's happening with the investigation of that swim coach."

"Well, the coroner's report is in, but you know these Chicago cops. Hold on to information like boa constrictors. Captain Gutierrez managed to snag a copy of the report though. He's still got friends downtown. Anyway, it seems like that coach had been dead for at least two hours before Alice showed up at the pool. Should clear her, though she hasn't been reinstated yet. Gutierrez needs to get the report officially and dot the 'i's' and cross the 't's'. But it's good news overall.

"Gossip mill says Alice has a lawyer now. Duty sergeant told me when he came in. Recognized him as a big-time lawyer by his shark suit. Had an appointment with the captain, actually, probably to see about getting her reinstated more quickly. I wonder if he'll be able to get some back pay for Alice. Still, she did leave, and that doesn't look good, so I don't know."

Oh, thank God, I was thinking. Alice called that lawyer.

"Kristin, you still there?" Mel said. I realized I needed to reply.

"That's really good news, Mel, considering. Could have been so much worse."

"Ain't that the truth?" he replied. "Listen, I gotta go. Kiss those babies for me."

"I will, Mel."

What a good guy he was and a good friend to Alice.

I'd forgotten all about the breast pump while I'd been talking to Mel. The light on the front had turned to red. I was finished.

I rang for a nurse to take the milk and refrigerate it. Time to give Tom a lesson in feeding tiny babies.

11

~

We shall not all sleep, but we shall all be changed.

—1 Corinthians 15:51

Three days later

"What time is it?" Tom mumbled as Natalie's wailing woke him.

I squinted at the bedside digital clock.

"Four am." I had already been waking. The fullness in my breasts was telling me there were babies to feed.

"Who gets what?" Tom said after pushing himself to a semi-sitting position on the side of the bed.

Where was my surgeon husband who could wake from a sound sleep in a second and prescribe a medication or treatment?

"Natalie gets the breast this time, Olivia gets the bottle," I said slowly so he'd take it in.

"Bottle, Olivia. Right."

Olivia was still sleeping but she needed to be awakened and fed. We were letting Natalie, the larger and more active twin, set the feeding schedule to make sure Olivia got enough. I pumped milk during the off times they weren't nursing, and we had plenty stored in the little bedroom refrigerator.

The kitchen was finished, all goddesses of the hearth be praised, and the spare bedroom had been turned back into a bedroom. Giles had volunteered to put everything away in the new kitchen, and since he'd helped design it, I was sure it would be a TV chef worthy space. Carol was allowed to help, but only under his guidance.

The nanny's rooms with the *en suite* bathroom were finished but the furniture had not yet been delivered.

Today, I thought as I took the screaming Natalie over to the changing table for a dry diaper. That furniture better get here today.

Across the room, Tom was crooning to Olivia while carrying her over to also get a dry diaper, but she was still dozing slightly, I could see.

Our whole bedroom had been turned into the twin's nursery. Gone was the equipment for my bedrest and in its place, there was a changing table, two bassinettes, and two rocking chairs, plus the little refrigerator and a bottle sterilizer.

Tom finished changing Olivia and placed her back in her bassinette for a moment while he dispensed a bottle of breast milk for her.

Tom had found this amazing device that kept the breast milk cold until you put a bottle underneath the spout and pressed a button. Then the milk would dispense, warmed to a preset temperature. It was kind of like a breast milk high end Nespresso machine but without the foam. It had cost a lot, and I'd been skeptical, but when I saw how Tom stumbled around in the middle of the night, I thought it was worth it.

Natalie had already latched on to my nipple and was getting right down to feeding. The nursing pillow we had could accommodate two on my lap, and sometimes during the day I did that, but at night it was good to let Natalie and Olivia go at their own paces.

"That's it, sweetheart," Tom was murmuring. "Open a little more. That's my princess. Now some sucking. Good, good."

At first the girls had been reluctant to take bottles from Tom.

"Take some of the breast milk and rub it on your chest," I'd advised him.

"You have got to be joking," he said warily.

"No, it works. They'll smell you and take the bottle."

It had worked, but Tom vigorously scrubbed his chest afterwards.

I just smelled like a milk dispensary all the time.

I went into a kind of nursing coma for a little while. Natalie needed no help from me. But after about a quarter hour, I opened my eyes to check on Tom and Olivia. It looked like they were both doing fine, so I let myself relax again.

We got back into bed after putting the twins in their bassinettes. I glanced at the clock. It was 4:50 am. They would want to eat again in two hours.

Tom lay back on his pillows, and I thought he was out like a light.

"When does the nanny start again?" he mumbled.

"Two days, Tom. Two days. Hang on."

* * *

Five days later

"The girls are settled in their nursery," Mrs. Brown said, bustling into my study room carrying the breast milk machine.

She was a sturdy, fireplug of a woman who seemed to dress exclusively in velour tracksuits and floral aprons. Her brown eyes peered through glasses that had sequined frames, and her shoes were sequined sneakers. She was no taller than Marco's mother, Natalie Ginelli, who didn't even come up to my shoulder, but like that adult Natalie, she had a very large presence. I had noticed Carol seemed very intimidated by her, but Giles had taken to her right away. I didn't know if Mrs. Brown had any Senegalese relatives, but I had heard her chatting away with Giles in the kitchen about a dish he was making.

Things were almost calm. Tom had left to "check on a few things at the hospital" in the late morning. I thought he just needed to get away for a little while. I knew how he felt.

After I had expressed the milk, I carried it and the machine into the new kitchen.

It really was spectacular. The custom off-white cabinets went all the way to the ceiling. A copper hood over the 8-burner stove gleamed. There was a huge island in the center of the room with stools on one side. It had a second sink and a second dishwasher!

The wood planked floors were picked up by some wood beams in the ceiling from which hung globe lights that had a lot of dimmer settings.

The open concept had been achieved by pushing out the back of the house both on the first floor and making room for the two bedrooms upstairs.

After the kitchen area proper, there was a plank table that sat 12 and could be extended to seat 16. Beyond that was a generous sized family room with couches, chairs, and a TV console over a gas fireplace. There were bookcases on either side. Molly had claimed the space in front of the fireplace for her own, and we had placed a dog bed there for her. She raised her head when I walked into the kitchen but then settled down and went back to sleep. These last weeks had tired her out too, I realized.

Mrs. Brown had set up a baby monitor at one end of the marble topped counter. She was just coming down the back stairs when I was putting the breast milk in the refrigerator.

"Now, now, I could have come get that from you. The less you exert yourself, the faster you will heal, you know," she said firmly.

I personally did not need a nanny.

"Thank you. I'm heading out for a walk. I'll be gone about an hour. You have my cell phone number, right?"

"Why, yes I do, but do you think . . ."

"Yes, I do," I interrupted.

I was already dressed in yoga pants (stretched a little tight in the middle) and an older, loose top. Thank you, Eileen Fisher. I grabbed my purse from my study room and slung it over a loose jacket from the front hall closet.

I headed for campus and my office. It was only a three-block walk. I wouldn't stay long, but I would breathe in the dust of our ancient building and the unwashed smell of students like an elixir. At least for a short while.

When I arrived at Myerson, the building where Philosophy and Religion was housed at the top, I briefly considered taking the rickety elevator. I decided to chance it since even walking the three blocks had been tiring.

As I stepped out on our office floor, I took stock of the changes to our cramped quarters.

Dr. Nia Zendaya Turner as a full professor had needed a decent office, and I must say converting the unused faculty secretary's space to that had been a good decision. The copier was housed in a closet next door.

I still shared an office, now with Dr. Sandra Ellen Parker, our new environmental ethics assistant professor. She was a quiet, efficient young woman, and I had no trouble sharing with her. I hoped she felt the same.

I saw Aduba Abubaker's door was open. He now occupied the office of Hercules Abraham, Emeritus Professor of Judaism who had graciously given the space up to him, though Hercules still taught one class.

"Hi, Aduba!" I called from the door. "Or should I say, 'Abbie?'" Marco's father had started calling Aduba "Abbie" last semester, and I'd been horrified. Aduba had said it was a good thing because he could introduce himself to Dr. Abraham's Jewish god as "Abbie" when he moved into that office and all would be well. Then he had laughed, and I had sighed with relief.

"Kristin! So good to see you up and around. How are the babies? How are you and Tom holding up? Two babies are a lot more than one," he noted, now not joking.

"All too true, Aduba. And I think Tom is finding out how hard it can be to take care of infants. Makes surgery look like a piece of cake."

"When will you be resuming your class?" he asked, gathering some materials, and heading for the door where I was standing.

"After Thanksgiving," I said, stepping back into the hall. "Nia's been subbing, and she's been great," I said.

"Yes, we did well with those two appointments," Aduba said. He crossed the hall and went into our largest classroom.

I saw Adelaide's door was partly ajar.

I stopped first at the wonderful coffee machine she had installed when becoming department chair and got myself a heavenly half a cup. Then I knocked on the partly open door.

"Come in," she called, and I pushed the door all the way open.

"Oh, Kristin. How nice. Come in and have a seat."

Adelaide had made a welcoming sitting area in her office, unlike her predecessor who had decorated for intimidation.

She frowned slightly at the coffee cup in my hand but didn't say anything.

"How are the girls?" she asked, and I passed over my phone and let her scroll through what seemed like the couple of thousand photos we had of them so far.

"They are great as you can see, and they've even gained some weight this first week."

In addition to all the other equipment we had in our bedroom, Tom had gotten a medical professional baby scale. He weighed them daily and kept a chart. Of course, he did.

I covered my mouth with my hand to unsuccessfully hide a yawn.

"Keeping you up at night?" Adelaide asked when my mouth was finally shut.

"Oh yes. And speaking of which, I better get back. The nanny is new, though she seems very competent."

"Oh, good. So, you still on schedule to resume teaching after Thanksgiving break?"

"Yes, I'm counting on it," I said with a chuckle.

Adelaide was not a hugger, but she patted me warmly on the back as I got up to leave.

By the time I got home, I was exhausted but feeling more like myself.

I checked with Mrs. Brown who said the girls had eaten "with no trouble at all." I looked in on them, and they were sleeping away.

I went down to our bedroom planning on taking a nap. When I opened the door, I saw Tom was flat on his back, out cold.

I crawled into bed next to him and did the same.

12

~

When healthy boundaries have been breached, we swing between hyperactivation, fight and flight responses, and hypoactivation, or freeze response, each with their own set of distinct symptoms.

—**Roland Bal**, *Resolving Trauma and PTSD*

I HAD BEEN TEXTING with Alice for the last two weeks, and we had finally made a plan to get together at the coffee shop she preferred on campus.

It was one of those Chicago fall days that are stunning with warm sunshine, a light breeze, and a sense of impending doom that weather like this would not be felt again for five or six months.

I had bundled the girls into the tandem stroller and headed toward campus, enjoying the sense of being out with them. I had walked marathons with the boys when they were babies. The fresh air did all of us a lot of good.

Now the boys were "big brothers," and they had gone through several stages with their new sisters. At first, they had been intrigued with how tiny the girls' hands and feet were. Then, I'd asked each boy to give a bottle. Natalie had been her customary aggressive self, latching on to the bottle and sucking vigorously. Olivia, always more likely to size a situation up before committing, had rubbed her face on the nipple of the bottle and fussed. I had matched sister up with similar temperament brother, giving aggressive eater Natalie to Sam to feed and "I like to think about it" Olivia to Mike. I'd explained each girl's preferences to the boys, and I must say it worked pretty well. Mike was patient with Olivia, and Sam and Natalie had gotten right down to her eating vigorously. But then the boys hadn't wanted to repeat the experience. Been there, done that.

"She eats kinda slow," Sam had said when the bottle was half empty.

"Well, babies have small stomachs and need to take their time," I said quietly from across the room. I was still "she who smells like milk" to the girls and my presence could mess up bottle-feeding in a second.

Still, it had been a good experience for the boys, I thought, though they made excuses when I was breast feeding to be elsewhere.

The family room was working great to bring us all together. The girls now had bounce chairs, and the boys would bounce them a little when they first came home from school.

Well, I thought, wait until they're crawling and getting into the boys' stuff. That would be another hurdle.

* * *

Alice and I were sitting outside in a patch of sunshine on the coffee shop patio. She had a cup of English Breakfast tea, and I had a half caffeine, half decaf blend that I must confess this shop did well.

She'd stayed with the girls while I'd gotten our drinks and had cocked her head at my small, cardboard cup. I was never going back to that hideous chamomile tea that I'd drunk when she and I were trying to give up caffeine and tobacco respectively. I had slid a little on the caffeine, it was true, and Alice had backslid on the smoking. I could smell it on her from across the small café table, but she only took out a stick of gum and twirled it like she used to do while quitting. I appreciated her not smoking around the girls.

"How many hours of sleep are you and Tom getting now?" Alice said, peering at me and then taking the lid off her tea and blowing on it.

"Oh, it varies, but it's now every three hours or so. Two days ago, they slept four hours straight at night, and I woke with a start worrying something was wrong."

"Yeah, yeah. You worry about them even when you're sleeping," Alice said slowly gazing down into her tea.

I thought she was talking about the threat of possible prosecution and her worry about her daughter, but I didn't comment.

"So, you're back on the campus police force full-time now? Mostly days?" I asked, though I actually knew that from Mel.

"Right. Days. And, well, I got the salary back for those days I was suspended. That Acosta, he's on stuff. Argued I didn't get some kind of process, and they shouldn't have done that without proof and all. He's good, Kristin, really good. And that detective, he keeps coming back at me, about every week now. Tryin' to find a way to say the coroner was wrong, or I left my recorder nearby so I could have an alibi, or whatever lie they can think of. And that lawyer, he just keeps shutting them down. I can't thank you . . ."

"You stop that," I said, cutting her off. "You saved me and the babies. We're quits, you hear, and I don't want any more of that."

"Yeah, yeah. I made a phone call for an ambulance," she said, glaring at me.

"Yeah, yeah, well I made a phone call to a lawyer, so there," I countered. Then I added, "Hey, we're almost back to arguing."

Alice chuckled a little, but it stopped almost immediately.

"You know, what would really help is finding out who killed that coach," I said. "That will shut that detective up for certain."

"Kristin, no. You can't be that much of an idiot to try that now. You've got these little ones, your boys, your teaching. Come on. Don't go there!"

A little fuss came from under the light blanket I had draped over the stroller. Alice automatically put a hand on the handle of the stroller and rocked it a little.

"I'm not planning on doing much," I said. "And I do need to get back into pre-baby shape. I thought I'd swim laps at that aquatic center when the current team is practicing. They keep two lanes for non-team members, and I've signed up for a lane two times a week. I start next week."

I took a sip of my coffee and then looked more closely at Alice. She had turned to face the bushes that surrounded the patio, and she was rigid. Absolutely rigid, her hands clenched in her lap and the tendons in her neck sticking out above the collar of her jacket.

What in the name of heaven was this?

"Alice?" I said softly, then a little louder.

No response.

I got up and went around to where she was facing. I crouched down and looked right into her face. It was blank. Just blank.

"Alice. Come on now. It's me, Kristin."

Then Natalie started to wail, and Alice's face grimaced.

"What the hell you doin' over here?" she demanded. "And can't you hear that baby?"

"You phased out there for a minute, Alice. Seriously. I was concerned," I said, getting up and going back to my chair.

"Don't get all crazy on me now," she said roughly. "I was just thinking."

Natalie's wails increased in volume, and Olivia woke up too. I knew it was time for them to nurse, but I was reluctant to let Alice leave without addressing the blanking out.

"You gotta feed those kids, and I gotta go. Don't worry about me." And she got up and nearly ran out the exit of the patio.

I rocked the carriage a little, and the wails subsided to snuffles and complaints. My milk started to let down, so I picked up Natalie and then Olivia and settled them under my jacket. Two quick pulls on the Velcro that held my nursing blouse together, and they started to settle down, suckling away. I scooted the chair up to the table so I could reach my coffee. We all three drank our beverages, but only I was deeply worried about Alice.

* * *

Alice made her way across the campus, following her usual route from east to west. There was a cloud on the western horizon now. Storms from the west could blow up quickly, and she hoped Kristin would get those babies home before that.

"Officer, officer," a female student ran up, her dreads flying every which way and her poncho nearly off one shoulder.

"A guy is using a hammer to damage bicycles chained up at the aquatics center. Hurry!"

Alice sprinted along behind the agitated student and saw about half a dozen bikes knocked over, though still chained to the large bike rack. A small group of students was standing around, of course videoing the scene on their cell phones, and tapping away on their screens, probably texting everyone they knew.

"So, what happened?" Alice asked as she came up.

The gaggle all tried to tell her at once.

"Tell you what. Who's got the best video of what happened?"

"Probably you, Harold," a young woman said, gesturing toward a serious geek in a torn anorak, wearing a worn backpack.

"Yeah. Probably I do. He was still whacking away at the bikes when I started filming."

He held his phone up and pressed play.

Alice saw a guy in a hoodie, probably white, with a hammer just going at one of the chained bikes until two male students yelled, "Hey, quit that you maniac," and the hoodie guy ran away.

"Email that to me, will you?" Alice asked, dictating her work email to him.

"Sure," Harold said and instantly complied.

"Anybody recognize that guy?" Alice asked the group, now dwindling in numbers as the excitement was over. And nobody wanted to be questioned.

Some head shaking followed and then most of them went their separate ways.

Alice took her own photos of the damaged bikes and emailed them to her work account.

What gets into people, she thought, as she put her phone back in her pocket.

Then she glanced up and saw the full sweep of the aquatic center in front of her, looming over everything, growing in size as it filled with water, its windows bulging, trying to hold in the flood.

She froze. Terrified.

"Officer! Officer! Are you okay?" a voice asked.

It sounded a long way off.

"Should I call 911?" the voice asked somebody.

No. No police. Not that. No.

Alice shook her head no. She couldn't speak.

"You're not having a stroke, or anything are you?" the second voice asked.

"No. Fine. Just go," Alice said in a monotone.

They moved away but stayed watching her.

I have to move, she thought. Get away from this building. Get away.

She turned on shaky legs and went back across the street to the path with her regular route. There was a bench. She remembered. Find the bench.

She saw it. Under a tree. She nearly collapsed on to it.

That counselor. That Shannon something. Gotta call her. I need help. Can't get suspended again.

Alice dug around in her inside jacket pocket where she'd put the papers Kristin had given her. She located them and dug out her phone. She dialed.

"Hello, this is Dr. Pearson Hill," a voice said.

"Dr. Hill?" Alice asked, her voice sounding like she was choking on each word.

"Yes, this is she. Are you in distress?"

"This is Alice Matthews and yes, yes I think I'm in distress."

"Tell me about it. I have time. Tell me now, and we'll work on it," Dr. Hill said.

Alice could barely hold herself to even sit upright as she felt the grip of the terror subside.

"I am freezing. Blanking out. Don't know for how long. A few times now. It's just a blank."

"Okay. Where are you?"

"I'm on the university campus."

"Walk over to the Emergency Room, and I'll meet you there. I'm in Hyde Park."

"Oh, no. Can't. I can't miss work," Alice stammered out.

"Officer Matthews, you are in distress, and you need medical help. It is not a disgrace, it is not shirking work, it just is what you are feeling right now. Will you go to the ER?"

"Okay. I guess. This is really stupid, this freezing," Alice said as she stood up on wobbly legs.

"It's not stupid. It's really very smart. You are trying to defend yourself, and freezing is one way to do that. There are better ways, but let's deal with this right now," Dr. Hill said.

"Okay," Alice said, but she didn't put the phone away. She held it out in front of her like she could follow it, and she turned toward the hospital. On the way she used her other hand to radio in that she was not well and heading to the ER.

"Copy that," the dispatcher said.

Sure, Alice thought. Copy that. Copy what?

13

Our [white Americans'] precarious position demands that we remain vigilantly ignorant of our own origin story. Up until very recently, history books have been full of the lies necessary to defend an impossibly innocent and glorious past."

— **Robert P. Jones, *The Hidden Roots of White Supremacy and the Path to a Shared American Future***

"**Emergency faculty meeting, 8:00** am Monday. Dr. Winters."

The text from Adelaide was not unexpected. Over the Thanksgiving holiday all hell had broken loose on campus over the title and content of my colleague, Nia Zendaya Turner's, class, "The Social Construction of Whiteness." That reference to "whiteness" as an object of inquiry, not the God-given privilege conservatives believed it was, had really gotten the campus right-wing crowd going. A well-known student conservative activist had put out a social media post claiming that "whites are under attack in academia" citing Dr. Turner's class by name. He also had given her campus phone number, email address and the address of her office. Our offices in Myerson to be specific.

I'd gotten the text on Sunday, Mrs. Brown's day off. But since she planned to return Sunday evening, I thought it would not be a problem to leave for campus before 8 am on Monday. I'd texted her anyway later in the day on Sunday, and she'd replied, "Not a problem."

Mrs. Brown was organized.

Tom was starting back to full-time surgery today as well. I got up when he did and went to get the girls so I could nurse them well before I left for the meeting. I had a peaceful time rocking and nursing while Tom moved quietly around our bedroom.

He kissed all three of us on the head, and when he saw both babies were finished, he picked up Olivia and sat down on the side of the bed to confidently hold her on his knee to pat her back so she would burp. Tom had learned a lot over the past few weeks. I did the same with Natalie. Two loud burps quickly followed. We both chuckled.

Tom carried Olivia back to the nursery, and I brought Natalie, and we placed them in their bassinettes. Tom left, and I stayed to confer with Mrs. Brown.

"I have this early meeting, but then I will come back home at lunch in time to nurse them again, or pump if they've had two feedings," I said, standing in the doorway.

"That will be very good," she replied. "We have more than enough breast milk stored, but it is important they also take the breast." She stood between the two bassinettes like she was guarding them. Why did I sometimes feel like there was a little power struggle with Mrs. Brown over the babies? I decided not to worry about it. She was doing a marvelous job from all I could see. I bid her good morning and left to take a shower. I was still thrilled at being able to shower.

The boys and I had a nice breakfast of Bori made by Giles. We sat at the breakfast counter and talked with Giles about the Thanksgiving meal. He had used a sweet and sour tamarind pulp, a prized ingredient in Senegal, where it is formed into candies, mixed into a cooling drink, or slathered over grilled fish. He'd made a glaze with it and some fish sauce for the turkey. Delicious, even without the chilis he'd wanted to add. I'd asked him to leave those off as I thought that might flavor my milk as well, and the girls would not like it. Sam wanted to know where Giles got his idea for cooking turkey like that.

"There's no Thanksgiving in Senegal, right?" he asked around a mouthful of Bori.

"Wait until your mouth is empty before you talk, okay Sam?" I said.

He made a show of swallowing and then drank a little milk.

Giles smiled.

"No, this Thanksgiving is only your holiday in this country. Where I come from, we have many holidays that center around food. We make a lot of food for our Christmas, how you say it, festin? Feast? Mostly chicken then." I knew that Giles and his family, as Senegalese Christians, had been persecuted as a religious minority.

Carol came down the back stairs to join us, but I realized I needed to get going. It was 7:45 already.

Finally, I was out the door and heading to the office.

I knew I would not see Alice on campus. I had heard from Mel about a week ago that she was taking a paid medical leave of absence. He didn't know exactly why, and I wasn't going to share with him what I'd seen about her brief freeze response to my talking about swimming laps at the pool. I was immensely glad she was getting a rest, and I suspected she had called my therapist friend.

Speaking of swimming, I thought as I hurried along, my first day having a reserved lane at the aquatic center was tomorrow. I would need to try on my largest bathing suit. I was not looking forward to that.

I reached Myerson and hurried up the stairs. I could hear voices down the hall in the large seminar room we used for faculty meetings. As usual, the voices were raised but I did not hear Adelaide calling for order. I snuck over to the coffee machine. I had brought my insulated cup in my bag, and I got half a cup of caffeinated and a half cup decaf. I would not count that other half cup of caffeinated I had at breakfast. I doctored the coffee and headed over to the seminar room.

Adelaide's door opened down the hall, and I slipped in, leaving the door ajar for her.

* * *

I paused as I walked toward the big seminar table we used for faculty meetings. Captain Gutierrez was seated at the head of it.

Serious business for him to come in person, I thought.

I nodded at him, and he nodded back.

Alfonso Gutierrez had come from Arizona and taken the position of captain of the campus police last year after the previous captain had left after exposing a big drug ring and a murder on campus.

Alice liked Gutierrez and had worried last spring he might leave, but here he was. His black hair, worn a little too long, had more gray in it than I remembered, as did his enormous mustache. His broad shoulders were very much in evidence as he sat at the end of the table, though I knew when he stood, he would barely reach five and a half feet. But he had a lot of presence.

As I placed my travel mug by an empty seat, I saw everyone else had a cup or mug in front of them except Captain Gutierrez. Was it a subtle message that he was not so welcome here, or had he already refused a beverage? Faculty tended to be skeptical at best toward the campus police. I ought to know. I was the representative to the joint faculty/campus police committee. We investigated complaints, and there were many. Some campus police grossly exceeded their authority and did hassle racial ethnic minority students on campus, stopping them repeatedly to check their student I.D.'s. I knew that directly from Giles. But some, like Alice and Mel, were very dedicated. I thought Gutierrez fit into the latter category.

"Good to see you Captain Gutierrez," I said warmly. "Could I get you a cup of coffee? I can assure you it is an excellent brew."

"Why yes," he replied in his slightly accented English.

I turned to go back out the door and Adelaide, who'd come in behind me, gave me a nod. I quickly returned with a cup of black coffee for Gutierrez, and his big mustache turned up at the edges as he thanked me.

I sat down and while I took a sip from my mug, I assessed the colleagues seated around the big table. The spaces were certainly filling up compared to when I'd first joined the faculty. Back then we had lost so many positions, some to resignation and one to death, the table had been nearly deserted even in meetings of the full faculty.

Adelaide Winters, as department chairperson and Professor of Women and Religion, had taken the seat at the other end of the table from Gutierrez. Her normal expression was serious, but today new lines seemed to have appeared in her forehead since I'd last seen her. She had on a lovely woven scarf over her customary flowing dress, but as I watched her she impatiently tugged it off and threw it on the table.

Next to her sat Donald Willie, Professor of Psychology and Religion. Unlike Gutierrez's lush mustache, Donald's was wispy and brown. It was likely sparse because he kept stroking it or pulling it when agitated. He alternated that with taking his horned-rimmed glasses off and gesturing with them. The mustache and glasses matched his wispy brown hair. He favored the tweed jackets with patches on the elbows and khaki pants of those men who want so much to look like academics. Donald was a study in wispy brown, and it fit his personality. I'd tried to warm up to him last semester, but he kept revealing himself as a coward and a mass of prejudices he unsuccessfully hid in liberal-sounding claptrap.

I did not like Donald.

Next to him was Aduba Abubakar, our Professor of Islam and Diaspora Studies. He was originally from Nigeria. His doctorate was from Oxford, and he was a brilliant guy. He had been viciously attacked by campus racists when he'd first joined us last year. He had stood up to the haters with dignity, but I wondered what toll this new crisis was having on him. I checked his cheek surreptitiously. His stress response was to chew on the inside of his cheek. So far, his face looked smooth. His son, who liked to be called Jack, was friends with my boys, and his teacup poodle, Hulk, was friends with Molly.

To my left was Sandra Ellen Parker, our new Assistant Professor of Environmental Ethics. She was a tall, thin woman with what I could only describe as a buzz cut. She seemed to dress exclusively in clothes and boots that looked like they had come from Patagonia, the South American country not the store. Everything she wore was well-worn. I knew from reading her work and listening to her lecture that she did extensive field work. For all I knew she was starting to do that in the Chicago area. She was a person of few words, but I had found her very pleasant as an officemate.

And just to the right of Gutierrez was Nia Zendaya Turner, Professor of African American Studies and Womanist Ethics. I thought the word to describe her was "distinguished." Not yet 40, she held both a BA and JD from Harvard, and then had a Ph.D. in Ethics from Claremont. I reminded myself of the apt title of her latest book, *Survive to Prevail: Womanist Ethics and the Politics of Death.* Based on what I'd heard about the threats against her from Adelaide, they were the epitome of the politics of death.

Gutierrez had been consulting some notes while he finished his coffee. He raised his head and looked around the table.

"As some of you know, Dr. Turner has been cyberbullied by a student here at the university and after his publishing her email address, phone number and office address, she has been bombarded with the vilest kinds of threats, including death threats."

I looked over at Nia and her hands were resting in her lap. She gave no overt sign of distress, but though she had researched the politics of death, being on the receiving end was something entirely different.

"So, after consulting with Dr. Winters," and Gutierrez nodded to Adelaide at the other end of the table, "here's what we are going to do. All your office doors will receive new keycard locks that will only open for your card."

I wondered if Gutierrez knew that all the doors on this floor opened with the same key. Well, that would change.

"All classroom doors will similarly be given keycard locks."

He glanced around the table; I thought assessing the response. No one spoke.

"Finally, security cameras will be placed in the stairway and the hall."

"Thank you, Captain Gutierrez," Adelaide said quietly. "Do you have any questions?" she asked the room.

"Why do we need to be spied on when she's the one who's getting the threats?" Donald huffed, nodding his head in Nia's direction.

"All of you are at risk at this point," Gutierrez replied levelly. "Extremists are not exactly careful when they physically attack. Mostly they just like to spout off hate on social media, but sometimes they do act. And they don't particularly care whom they hurt in the process."

Donald's pasty, white skin turned even whiter.

"Well, it's obvious we need to move her office someplace else," he said in a clipped tone.

"That's enough, Dr. Willie," Adelaide said sternly. "If you are uncomfortable being here, work from home."

"I have a question," Aduba said in his British accented voice into the silence that followed Adelaide's stern admonition to Donald. "Who will review the tapes, and who will be assessing the threat, as you say?"

"I will review the tapes, and they will not be available to anyone else unless there is an incident," Gutierrez said.

"Yes, Dr. Parker," Adelaide said. I hadn't noticed she was raising her hand.

"Why has this student not been expelled?" she asked reasonably. "Such conduct surely must violate several academic standards."

"Well," Adelaide sighed. "Not here. Dr. Turner has complained to the administration, and, here I don't want to speak for you, Dr. Turner, but since the university published its 'Free Speech Principles' in 2014, such behavior, the administration is claiming, is covered under that policy as free speech." She paused. "I think this policy is deeply misguided and should be repealed, but there it is. The administration has refused to take action against the student. The best we can do is try to protect Dr. Turner."

I strongly opposed the so-called "Free Speech Policy," and I had a statement on each syllabus I gave out indicating how my classes would be structured to prevent bullying and give each person space to leave if they felt threatened or uncomfortable. White Americans tended to see unfettered "free speech" as the free exchange of ideas. They were incredibly ignorant about how much verbal abuse and threats racial/ethnic minorities faced, sometimes on a daily basis. In short, I thought the university's policy was the very definition of the "construction of whiteness."

No one else had spoken while I was musing so I turned toward Nia.

"Dr. Turner," I asked, looking down the table at her. "Does this plan meet with your approval?"

Nia looked around the table.

"I have agreed to the plan, though I am thinking about possible legal actions that it might be wise for me to take. I have been talking with other legal scholars about how we effectively make it very financially painful for those who engage in cyberbullying. And," she added pointedly, "those who protect it."

I remembered Nia was a lawyer as well as a Ph.D. in ethics.

"Good idea," I said.

Captain Gutierrez took out some cards and had us pass them around the table.

"You will see I have inked in my cell number on the back. Anything you want to discuss or report to me, just give me a call."

Adelaide thanked him, and he left.

"Well," she said, looking around the room. "Keep your eyes and ears open, that's what I advise."

"Intolerable," Donald muttered, shoved his chair back, and hustled from the room.

I waited until Nia stood, and I moved next to her.

"Do you have time to talk about our classes now, or can we schedule a time?" I asked.

"I have a student tutorial now, but I could meet for coffee this afternoon," she said.

"Excellent. You know that coffee shop in the basement of the divinity school building?"

"'Where God Drinks Coffee?'" she chuckled. "Yes, I do. Let's say 3."

"Great. And Nia, you know I was a cop before I started to teach religion. Whatever you need, if it's a bodyguard or coffee and conversation, let me know."

She laughed again.

"Didn't you just have twins?"

I laughed too and then said seriously, "There's a lot I can still do, and I'll help you if I can."

She looked at me for a long moment and then said, "Well, I believe that." And she turned and headed toward her office.

I headed out and called Kelly.

"What are you hearing about this cyberbullying?" I asked her.

"Yeah, well, it's a super mess, isn't it?" she said. "Listen, I have class now, but I could come by the house for lunch. We can talk then."

"Perfect," I said and disconnected.

It would be good to talk with Kelly, but I wished Alice were around to discuss this.

I walked home, feeling how the chill wind from the west was signaling the end of the nice fall days.

14

Cyber bullies can hide behind a mask of anonymity online and do not need direct physical access to their victims to do unimaginable harm.

– Anna Maria Chavez

I got home in time to start the girls on some tummy time on a playmat on the floor of their nursery. It was amazing how much they grew and changed each day. They were both trying to lift their heads already. I lay on the floor in front of the mat and watched them. Pretty soon though, there were grunts and complaints, and I turned them over to watch a free-standing mobile of stuffed animals.

They kicked and wiggled, but then Natalie started to fuss, and Olivia took her cue and chimed in. I glanced at my watch. We were inching toward a schedule, and it was almost noontime.

I carried the girls like little footballs into our bedroom, changed them and then settled down in a rocker with a nursing pillow.

I heard the front door open and a "Hi, Mom!" from Kelly.

"I'm up in our bedroom feeding the girls," I called.

Then there was some conversation, likely with Mrs. Brown, and I heard Kelly coming up the stairs. When she entered the bedroom, she was carrying the large cup with a lid and straw I used for my protein shakes. I was burning through calories with feeding the two babies, and I also really needed to stay hydrated. Mrs. Brown had likely been on her way to give it to me and asked Kelly.

Kelly held the cup where I could take several long drinks while still nursing the girls. I used to hate the taste of the brewer's yeast that I used with the dairy-free protein and soy milk. A little frozen soy ice cream made it fairly palatable, however.

When I nodded I'd had enough for the time being, Kelly moved the shake cup over to the table we'd kept in the bedroom.

"How are you doing and how are the girls?" she asked, gazing down at them.

"I think we're all good," I said. "They eat well, and we are getting on a schedule. Important to establish that with my going back to teaching."

"Well, you look great," Kelly said, sitting down in the other rocker.

I thought I looked okay when I consulted the mirror, but I still had bags under my eyes, and I certainly jiggled around the middle when I walked.

"Thanks, and you look very well yourself," I said, and it was true. She had slimmed down over the last years, adding long muscle instead of starving herself like so many young girls did. With her brown hair with auburn highlights, clear skin and always alert gaze, she was turning into such an attractive person, inside as well as outside.

"Thanks, I think Zeke thinks so too," she said a little shyly.

Ah, the sparkle in her eyes was romance, I thought.

"Could you give me another drink of the shake?" I asked, both because I needed it and because I wanted to think about how to pose my questions.

As I drank, though, I realized the girls were mostly finished. It would be better to have this conversation over lunch.

I handed Natalie over to Kelly to burp, and I took Olivia. Then we carried the sleeping babies down to the nursery where Mrs. Brown was rearranging the changing table.

"Good feeding," I told her. "I think they'll be fine until about 3:30 or 4."

"We'll see," she commented and went on folding receiving blankets. We did go through an astonishing number of those small, soft blankets.

"We're going to fix some lunch downstairs," I commented. "Can I bring you anything?"

"No, thank you, I went down and fixed a sandwich while you were nursing. I will eat that here while the girls sleep." She nodded complacently at the two bassinettes.

"Well, good," I commented. Mrs. Brown was not one for chit chat, I had noticed.

Kelly and I went down the back stairs.

"I just love this part of the house now!" she exclaimed as we came into spacious room. "Honestly, I thought you were crazy to try this construction over the summer, but it's worked out so well! I want a kitchen/family room like this when I have a house!"

She did a pirouette in the space between the center island and the big table, looking like Julie Andrews in "The Sound of Music."

I laughed.

"Okay, but let's not get ahead of ourselves. Lunch first."

We pulled our favorite cold cuts out of the refrigerator and fairly shortly had two big sandwiches on plates. Kelly got herself some water, and I had brought my shake. I had only finished half so far.

"So, Kelly, two things. First, I'd like to know what students think about this cyberbullying of Dr. Turner."

She chewed and took a sip of water.

"Well, my friends think that guy who posts the stuff about her class is a dweeb and a real jerk. He just does it to make himself seem important."

She paused.

"But around the edges you can hear people wondering if maybe he's got a point, that targeting being white, as opposed to targeting racism, isn't maybe going too far. And, of course, there are those students, and I suspect some faculty, who agree with him, frankly."

It was as I had surmised. It was one thing to criticize 'those racists over there' and another to be asked to examine your own white privilege. For those who were privileged enough to be studying at such an elite school, that had to make white people feel uncomfortable.

It's hard for those who have never even thought about their being white to experience that discomfort as a good thing.

I shared those thoughts with Kelly and asked her to keep me posted on what she heard.

"What does Zeke think?" I asked. Her boyfriend from high school who also went to the university was African American.

"Well, he's super tired of being asked to show his student I.D. on campus, I'll tell you that. There are campus cops that I know recognize him, and they do it anyway."

Something to bring up to my committee, I thought, though I'd leave Zeke's name out of it.

"But what he's said about the class is 'about damn time.'"

"I think so too, Kelly. I also wanted to ask you about what you are hearing about that swim coach who was drowned. What are people saying about that?"

"Well," she said slowly, "there's a girl who lives down the hall from me who said she had been considering leaving the team because that coach was a little too 'handsy,' if you know what I mean, and nobody ever went to the showers alone. But Kristin, I thought they had a suspect, and besides, what does Alice say?"

"That's helpful information Kelly. What's the name of the girl in your dorm?" I said as neutrally as I could, but what I was thinking was I knew it!

"She's a freshman. Her name is Katie Boen, she's from LA, some suburb, I think. Huge into swimming so it was really a shock to hear her say she was thinking of quitting the team. But really, Kristin, what about Alice?"

Kelly was too sharp. She wasn't going to just let her question slide.

"Alice is on a medical leave of absence, Kelly. And as far as I know, the Chicago police have no viable suspects."

I paused.

"I'm going to start swimming laps tomorrow to get in shape. I've reserved a lane when the team is practicing. I assume they'll have some kind of assistant coach fill in. I want to get to know the lay of the land."

"Does Dad know?"

"You mean does he know I'm swimming? I haven't brought it up specifically, no," I said in as casual a tone as I could muster.

"Oh, Kristin," Kelly sighed. "You don't change, do you?"

No, I thought. I don't change, and I like myself the way I am very much.

But I just smiled up at Kelly as she cleared her lunch plate, and I followed her out to the front hall.

"So, Kelly," I said as she was pulling on her pea coat, "could you tell Katie Boen I'd like to talk to her?"

"Sure," she said, but I could see I'd disappointed her by the slump of her shoulders.

"Thanks," I said and just kept quiet. But then I thought, I'd better tell Tom I was swimming. Kelly was sure to blab to him.

* * *

A little before 3 I climbed the stairs to our offices in Myerson. No more rickety elevator for me, I thought smugly.

I approached my office and saw the swipe card device had already been installed, but luckily the door was slightly ajar.

Sandra was at her desk with a photo of a desiccated forest on her screen. She had the outer cubical in our shared space, and the screen faced the door. I didn't know how she could stand focusing on what we were doing to the planet day after day. But I was glad for her work. She turned when she heard me.

"Hello, Kristin. So glad to see you back in the office."

"Thanks, it feels good to be here," I said. "I see we got the card swipe."

"Yes, we did. Yours is on your desk."

"Pretty efficient," I remarked as I headed for the room divider. "Unusual here, actually."

"They're in an uproar over in administration, I heard," she said as I picked up my card and walked back around the divider to the side of her desk.

"Really? I mean I assume so, but you're plugged into the gossip network pretty quickly."

"Old girls network," she said and her tanned face broke into a grin. "Mate of mine from Smith works in admin here. We connected right away."

"I keep up with some of my classmates from Smith as well. Seven Sisters rule!" I said holding up my hand, and we high fived. We had a nice few minutes figuring out when we had overlapped. Sandra had been a freshman when I had been a senior.

"Well, I have a meeting with Nia," I said, pocketing my new keycard.

"I'm out of here. I'm heading to the Indiana Dunes to examine erosion along the shore."

"I won't say 'have fun,' but I hope it is productive."

"Me too," she said as she shut down her computer, and the dying trees disappeared.

I headed across to Nia's office and knocked.

"Who is it?" I heard her say. Wise of her to check.

"Kristin," I called out, and I heard her come across the floor to unlock the door.

I entered and shut the door securely behind me. She headed toward the back wall. I saw she had made a small sitting area in the rear corner of the space that used to be the faculty secretary's office, back when we'd had a secretary for the department. That kind of support was gone forever in academics. Or at least for the humanities. Economics professors probably each had their own secretary.

Nia sat, and I saw she'd placed a vacuum carafe on the coffee table and a few of what looked like cinnamon rolls, only smaller and flatter.

"Coffee?" she asked hospitably and when I nodded, she filled a cup for me and did the same for herself.

"Have a cookie," she said, gesturing to the plate. "When I'm upset, I bake, and I've been baking a lot. Take two, in fact, take three. I'm preparing too many of my Mama's favorite recipes and then eating the results."

I looked at her still willowy figure and smiled, but I did take two of the delicious looking cookies.

"I'll tell you, Nia, I could, in fact, eat them all as the twins are nursing very well, and I burn about 2,000 calories a day just from that."

I munched away while Nia brought me up to speed on her guest lectures in "Religion in America."

"I think, after the cyberbullying became so well known, all the students were afraid to engage with me. I think they didn't want to be seen as part of the prejudiced mob. So, it was me lecturing them about the Civil Rights leaders and their silently taking notes." She grimaced.

"I'm sorry about that, Nia. I was just talking to a student, and she was saying that a lot of white students don't know how to feel, so they kind of default to a 'let's not keep stirring stuff up and get back to normal and just go on with our studies.' For them, it seems to me, normal is, of course, unexamined whiteness, but they're not questioning that."

"Yes, right," Nia said. "The cocoon of whiteness is very alluring and when stressed at all, whites will quickly revert." I nodded.

"So," she said, changing gears, what do you have in mind for your guest lecturing in my class?"

"I thought I would cover Civil Religion and the work that has been done on that since the Robert Bellah's *Civil Religion in America*. Amazing that was published in 1967 with all that was going on in terms of racial protest at the time. But while Bellah thought racism was a stain on the American character, he had set it aside as not fundamental to the kind of glue that holds a nation together in terms of its unifying and transcendent purposes."

"Good. Good. And where will you conclude that?" Nia had picked up a small pad and was making notes.

"Well, I think up until exactly now. Have you read Robby Jones latest, *The Hidden Roots of White Supremacy and the Path to a Shared American Future*? I think a case can be made that whiteness is a key pillar of American Civil Religion, not the 'sin' that Bellah and others after him have assumed, effectively sidelining it."

I took a bite of another of the cinnamon roll cookies and washed it down with a sip of coffee while Nia was writing.

She looked up, smiled a little at where the plate of cookies now held only crumbs, and nodded.

"Yes, that will work very well. It is the change of mindset that is so crucial in whiteness studies. How has it been constructed and reinforced so well as to both run the nation in many ways and yet be almost invisible to those doing the running?"

She examined her notes again and then got up and went to her desk computer.

"You can do two lectures, correct?"

"Yes, I think I can. What dates did you have in mind?" I reached down into my purse, pulled out my phone and opened the calendar app. We applied ourselves to finding suitable dates and then closed our electronics.

"So, now how are your babies? I made the mistake of telling Mama my colleague has twins, and now I will never hear the end of it."

Since I still had my phone in my hand, I passed it over, open to the photos. The pictures of today's tummy time had come out very well.

* * *

I got home just as the girls were waking up, and I was able to get them and head down to our bedroom to nurse them again. My memory of the boys as infants had faded a little, but it seemed to me that the girls were getting on a schedule much sooner. Or was it that I was a more experienced mother? Perhaps.

I heard the front door slam and the boys yell, "Mom! We're home!"

"Great!" I called back. "I'm upstairs nursing the girls. Come on up."

There was some muted conversation and then Sam called, "It's okay, we got lots of homework. We'll get started in the kitchen."

The nursing Mom was still an embarrassment.

When I finished, I carried the girls back into the nursery for a nap. I liked to have them awake and in their bounce chairs during dinner, but that wasn't for two hours.

I went back to our room and took a quick shower and then called Mel.

I told him I was going to swim tomorrow morning when the team was practicing and about Katie Boen, the swimmer who had called the coach "handsy" and who had almost quit the team.

"Excellent, Kristin! First lead I've heard of. The investigation is kind of stalled. Call me after and we can compare notes, not that I have any notes to speak of."

"Sure, Mel," I said, grateful for his enthusiasm at my initiative in swimming with the team.

But later that night, Tom was not at all enthusiastic when I told him I would start swimming when the team practiced.

"You have got to be kidding! Other people can do this now."

And the conversation went downhill from there.

Afterwards it had taken four chocolate truffles to calm me down.

15

~

You know my method. It is founded upon the observation of trifles.

—Arthur Conan Doyle, "The Boscombe Valley Mystery: A Sherlock Holmes Short Story,"

Tom was moving quietly around the bedroom assembling keys, wallet, hospital pass card, I.D. and so forth. I could tell from the set of his shoulders he was still not happy with me for pursing the investigation into who had killed the swim coach at the university.

I was rocking and nursing the girls so I could get to the pool to start swimming at 7:30 am. Right now, it wasn't seeming that great an idea to me either. I dozed a little as they suckled.

"So long. I don't think I'll be late tonight," Tom said from the doorway.

"Okay," I said sleepily. He often said he thought he wouldn't be late until he was.

I looked down. The girls were both asleep. I lay Natalie down on the bed while I burped Olivia, and then I switched. I used the football carry to take them down to the nursery. They stayed asleep as I placed them each in their bassinettes.

Mrs. Brown was up and dressed. I had cleared my exercise schedule with her in advance. She followed me out into the hall.

"Will you be home to nurse them at lunch?" she whispered.

"Yes," I said. "I'll call if anything happens to mess that up, but I don't anticipate that."

"Good, good," she said softly. She glanced back into the room. "They are progressing so nicely." She paused. "This is my first time caring for twins. I must say it is a little more challenging, but they coordinate with each other very well."

"Yes, it is challenging," I said smiling, "but I am glad you are with me for this. With the boys, I was on my own with a little help from my husband and some from his mother."

She patted my arm and turned back to the girls.

Ah, a little breakthrough with Mrs. Brown.

* * *

I had hoped to get to the pool while the team was still changing, but I was late, having driven over. "Hyde No Park" was living up to its name, and even though I had a parking sticker, I had had to wedge my Subaru into a space only about 6 inches longer than the car. Good thing I had mostly grown up in New York City and learned to drive there. New Yorkers prided themselves on being able to shoehorn their cars into too small spaces.

I was wearing my swimsuit under my clothes, so I was able to get ready quickly. The aquatic center was new and the lockers pristine. The remembered chill of pool locker rooms was the same. I shivered as I collected my cap and goggles, and I studiously avoided looking at myself in the long mirrors. I hurried out to the pool.

I had been able to get a list of the team members from the university athletics website, but they were already pounding up and down the lanes reserved for team practice. Kelly had arranged with Katie Boen to go for coffee with me after practice. I had mostly memorized the names, years, and home states from the list, so I'd have a place to start with her.

I pulled on my swim cap and positioned the goggles over my eyes. I went over to the lane I'd been assigned, waited for a clear space, and dove in. The shock of the cold water pierced me from head to foot. I was surprised my heart didn't stop. I surfaced and started the crawl, bent on nothing now but warming up. Soon the rhythm came back to me, and I slowly felt life and warmth return to my body. I swam for about half an hour according to my waterproof watch, and then pulled myself out of the pool. Enough for the first time exercising after giving birth.

I grabbed my towel off the bench where I'd left it and vigorously rubbed myself. Then I practically ran to the showers and let hot water do the rest in warming me up.

Since the team was still practicing, I had plenty of time to wait for Katie and also nose around. A young woman who must be the assistant coach was shouting instructions to various swimmers. She was stick thin and well-muscled. I could actually see the 6-pack of her abdominal muscles through the tight, maroon swimsuit with the university logo on the front. Her short, cropped hair was orange and stuck straight up above a hairband. She reminded me of that Muppet character Beaker, with his thin body and orange tuft of hair. As she strode along the side of the pool yelling at one swimmer or another, her hair hardly moved. Amanda Parkinson was her name. She had gone to New Trier high school on the northside of Chicago and then had coached their high school team until she was recruited here. She reminded me of a tightly coiled spring, topped with a tuft of orange. I wondered just how tightly wound she was and if she had finally snapped at the "handsy" coach.

There was another twenty minutes of practice, so I walked around, poking into the side rooms past the locker room. One labeled "storage" was indeed storage with racks that held various chemicals, a long hose, and some mops.

Another room held two weight benches, weights, a rowing machine, and a fixed rack to do pull ups. I wandered over to the weights. The lower weights were different colors. All were neatly racked except there didn't seem to be any eight-pound weights. The rack held 15, 12, 10, and then went to two sets of 5. I knelt to see if the 8's were under the rack, and I spied a purple weight pushed up right against the wall. I pulled it out. It was one of the two missing 8's. But search as I might, I did not find its mate.

The door opened, and Coach Parkinson and about half the team started to come in.

"This room is reserved for the team," the coach said through clenched teeth.

"Oh, that's okay," I said slowly, watching her. "I am new to the facilities and was just checking this room out."

"Okay, well, fine, but you need to leave now," she said, standing to the side so I could pass.

"Where is the other 8-pound weight?" I asked softly as I passed her.

She blanched and turned her head away.

As I stood in the pool area waiting for Katie Boen, I imagined that 8-pound weight being swung and connecting with the coach's head and him toppling into the water.

* * *

I led Katie to my car and cranked up the heat.

"Where do you like to have your coffee? I can drive us there and then drop you back where you need to be," I said as I rocked the car back and forth to get it out of the tiny space.

"How about the Commons?" she said, naming a coffee shop around the corner from where I lived.

"Great," I said and started to drive over there, spending a few moments imagining their croissants. Then I yanked my mind back to this investigation.

"Chicago must be a huge change from LA," I said, glancing over at her still tanned face as I drove.

"Oh, wow, is it. Nothing like I imagined," she said, fiddling with her gloves. "I just can't warm up to this place, you know? It's so grey, so cold, and really the people are too."

I grabbed a parking space as someone pulled out, so I didn't reply right away.

"Sounds like you're not happy with your choice of school?" I said as I held the door for her.

"I'm thinking about it," she said slowly as we wound our way to a scarred table. A server bustled right up. Katie ordered tea, and I asked for a coffee and croissant. I figured with swimming and nursing, I deserved it. I did immediately drink the large water the server had put down.

"What do you think of the team?" I asked, watching her shred her paper napkin.

"Well, they're all over the place," she said, her blue eyes hooded and her head bent.

"In what way?" I asked as she fell silent.

"Well, Sandy, that is, Sandy Samuels, she's from Michigan, and she made state there. She's a junior, and she knows what she's doing. But Anna Vovk, who's a freshman, has just recently been sponsored as an immigrant from Ukraine and honestly, she doesn't know much about swimming. I mean, I'm sure she's suffered and all, but really. I think her sponsor is a famous Chicago mucky muck who has a lot of clout at the university. And maybe it's good you know? Help someone who's been in a war?"

She paused, clearly thinking.

"Now Adrianna Sanchez, she's from the southside suburbs here, Midlothian I think, and it's clear she's had good coaching. Her Mom pushes her, I think. Her Mom works as office manager in Central Administration here and is over at the pool all the time when we're practicing. I'll bet she'll never miss a meet when those start. Totally into her daughter swimming. Really driven woman."

The server brought our drinks and my croissant, and I contemplated whether I should just ask straight out about the coach. I took a big drink of coffee and decided I should.

"Listen, Katie, Kelly told me you said the coach, the one who died, was 'handsy.' What did you mean by that?"

Katie turned white under her tan and further shredded her napkin. Then she spoke in almost a whisper.

"He was a big reason I have been thinking of transferring. I mean, I couldn't believe it. A few weeks ago, about two weeks before he died, I pulled myself up out of the pool, and he extended a hand to me to help me get up. His other hand, away from where the girls still in the water could see, stroked down from my back right to my butt crack, and he squeezed. I yanked my hand out of his, stepped back and said something like 'no you don't, you creep,' and he looked really angry. I called my parents that night and said I might like to transfer."

She was breathing hard.

"Here, take a sip of your tea," I said. "In fact, put a little sugar in it," and I pushed the sugar bowl over to her. She put a teaspoonful in the tea, stirred and took a sip.

"Look, he was a creep. You were right," I said firmly. "And if he was a creep with you, I bet he hit on other team members too."

"Yeah, well, I think he did." She took another drink. "And there was this 'don't go in the shower room alone' thing a couple of people said to me when I first started on the team. I asked why, but they just changed the subject. I mean, why do people put up with stuff like that? Why don't they report it and get rid of the guy?"

I didn't point out to her that she hadn't reported it, she'd just contemplated transferring.

"What about your assistant coach, Amanda Parkinson? Do you think he hit on her?" I asked while I casually took another bite of croissant to lower the emotional tone. Croissants send a low stress message, I think.

"I don't know her hardly at all," Katie said. "She's really tense and anxious all the time, I can tell you that."

She started to gather up her things, preparing to leave.

"Katie, are there other team members you think I should talk to?" I asked as she stood up.

"Well, don't bring my name into it, but I think Paige Walsh. She's a senior, a transfer from Northwestern. She really knows her stuff, and I just got the impression the coach was a little intimidated by her. And that goes for Alex Smith too. She's from Iowa and was state champion. She doesn't seem to take guff off of anybody.

I made a note of the names and thanked her.

"Do you want a ride anywhere?" I asked as I rose.

"No, no thanks. I'd rather walk. I have a lot of thinking to do."

I walked her out and when we were alone on the sidewalk, I turned to look directly at her.

"Katie, go to a counselor. Talk about what the coach did to you. Don't try to just 'forget it and move on.' It will stay with you and be harmful, okay?"

She didn't reply.

I pulled out a card and a pen from my purse. I quickly wrote my cell phone number on the back of it.

"There's my cell. If you think of anything else or want to talk, just give me a call. And really, talk to a therapist."

She pocketed the card.

"Thank you," she said and walked quickly away.

I watched her leave and wondered if she'd see a therapist. The odds were not good. I did think the university would soon see the back of her.

That was something to check, I thought suddenly. How many members of the swim team had quit the team and/or transferred out of the school in recent years?

I drove home and put the car in the garage. It did not make sense to drive around the university.

16

First, the physiological symptoms of post-traumatic stress disorder have [to be] brought within manageable limits. Second, the person [becomes] able to bear the feelings associated with traumatic memories.

— **Judith Lewis Herman**, *Trauma and Recovery*

SH: First, what we'll do today is just check in with how you're feeling. Have you had any reactions to the medication?

AM: I just don't like taking pills. I should be able to handle this myself.

SH: But you are taking them?

AM: Yeah, yeah.

SH: So how do they make you feel?

AM: Like I have a veil over my head. I can sort of see and hear people but it's all muted and blurry.

SH: That's normal when you're taking anti-depressants. Have you had any more of the freezing attacks?

AM: No. That's good, right? But I can't live like this. Even Shawna noticed I'm out of it most of the time.

SH: What did she say?

AM: Mama, you got a cold or somethin'? You look like you feeling bad.

SH: What did you say?

AM: I said I was sick but getting better.

SH: Well, that's the truth. And you will get better. I promise you, if you stick with this, you will start to feel better and finally recover.

AM: I don't honestly believe that.

SH: I know you don't. Not yet.

AM: (silence)

SH: You're at a point with the medication where we could try a little recovery work. Do you want to try?

AM: What's that? What's it like? (breath becomes more rapid)

SH: You tell me one memory, and I help you work through it.

AM: (breathing even harder)

SH: Let's get your breathing under control first. Breathe in for six counts, hold for four, and then out for six counts.

AM: (breathing)

SH: Good, good. Now hold on to that control and tell me one memory.

AM: I'm in the showers. Alone. He comes and looks at me. I see him and grab for my towel, but he takes it first. He just stares at me while I try to cover myself with my hands. Then he turns and walks out, taking my towel. (rapid breathing)

SH: Very good. Very good. Now just return to the controlled breathing. Six in, hold for four, and six out. That's it. Bring it under control. All the control belongs to you now. He doesn't control you. You are in control.

AM: (sputtering) Doesn't feel like it.

SH: We'll wait until it does feel like you have control. Keep breathing.

AM: (breath evens out)

SH: Let's try it again. Tell me.

AM: I'm in the showers . . . .

17

~

Never forget that justice is what love looks like in public.

— **Cornel West**

I PARKED MY CAR in my own garage. Probably the last parking space in Hyde Park. It was still just mid-morning. I checked in with Mrs. Brown upstairs, and the girls were sleeping soundly. I whispered I'd do some work downstairs, give them a late morning feeding and head back to campus. She nodded. Still no chit chat from Mrs. Brown.

At around 11, I went in to get the girls and feed them while I drank one of my protein drinks. They nursed well and, when I brought them back to the nursery, they were in a wakeful mood, kicking their legs and looking at their bassinette mobiles. I left them with a pang.

Early evening had become play time for them with the family. Well, except for Tom as he didn't always make it before they crashed, but sometimes he did and then he went back to the hospital for evening rounds.

I bundled up against the December weather and started to walk to campus. I thought I'd better call Mel about meeting Katie Boen. He picked up immediately.

"How'd it go?" he said. I realized he'd been waiting for my call, and I regretted not calling him sooner.

"Early days, but I do think that schmuck swim coach Larsen was abusing young women on this university swim team. I mean, Katie Boen told me about him helping her out of the pool and running his hand down her back to her butt crack where the other swimmers couldn't see. I wouldn't be surprised if she just transfers back to her home state."

"These guys are really the limit," he sputtered. "When I think of our kid being old enough to play on a team, I get freaked."

"Well, a good source, I think, will be the mother of another one of the team members. The young woman is a freshman and apparently her mother has started coming to observe all the practices. Did she see some behavior by the coach that worried her? Did the kid say anything that made her mother nervous about the coach? I've got a lecture at 1, but I plan to try to see the mother afterwards. Apparently, the mother works here in administration."

I stopped to sit on a bench in the main quadrangle. I was starting to breathe heavily from the morning's exertion. Bed rest had done a real number on my muscles.

"Who's the kid?" Mel asked.

"Adrianna Sanchez," I said, still breathing hard.

"Could be her mother is Janice Erika Sanchez. She's the manager of human resources. She has a good reputation. Tough job, that one."

"Good to know. Another thing, Mel. When I was in the aquatic center, I went by their small weight room. The hand weights were missing the 8's. An extra set of 5's had been filled in. I looked under the weight rack and one 8 was under it, pushed back against the wall. I was wondering if perhaps the coach had tried to assault some team member in that room, and she had grabbed one of the 8's to defend herself. If she'd swung it at the coach, it could have connected with his head. Then she could have dragged him to the pool and toppled him in."

That scenario had been keeping me up last night. I could almost see it in my mind's eye.

"Well, well, well," Mel said slowly.

"I think a search in those bushes and trees behind the aquatic center might be a good idea."

"You're right there, but I should do it, not the Chicago cops. I wanted to tell you that Captain Gutierrez spoke to me and said that Chicago detective came by his office, oh so solicitous about Alice and wanting to get access to her medical records with that therapist she's seeing in case, and I quote, 'she's a danger to herself.' Gutierrez blew him off, but you can see they have nothing and still have Alice in their sights."

Oh God. I wondered how likely it was that detective could succeed. All the trust in a therapist someone needed to recover could be destroyed if they did that. I thought I'd ask Tom tonight how likely that was to be able to happen.

"Kristin, you still there?" Mel asked.

"Yes, I just am so horrified by what you're saying. And you're right, you should be the one to look. Do you even know if the Chicago cops did a sweep outside the aquatic center? After all, they missed the single weight rolled under the weight rack."

"I don't know, but I can get over there this afternoon," he said. "And here's what I've found out. One of the young women who had been on the swim team committed suicide two years ago. Her father works in engineering here. I heard he was ranting and raving to anyone who would listen how it was the university's fault, and they should have protected his daughter better. I'm going to try to go talk to him."

"Good plan. I plan to call Ms. Sanchez when I get to my office and set up an appointment after I give this lecture. I'll call you after," I said, getting up to walk the last yards to Myerson.

"Okay," he paused. "Have you heard from Alice? I haven't."

"No, I haven't either. I hope she's okay, but I've thought giving her space was the best thing I could do."

As I trudged up the stairs toward my office, I heard Mel sigh and then softly say, "Me too." And he disconnected.

I swiped my keycard and entered my office. Sandra wasn't there, but there was a nice screensaver of whales jumping out of the ocean. I was glad she didn't focus all the time on the destruction of the planet, though her work still must be very hard to take.

I dropped my things at my desk, looked up the campus extension for Ms. Sanchez and dialed. An assistant answered and quickly scheduled me to see Ms. Sanchez at 3 pm. Clearly Ms. Sanchez ran an efficient office.

I gathered up my notes for the guest lecture in Nia's class and headed down the hall, coffee cup in tow. I fixed my (now) usual half caffeine, half decaf and entered the big seminar room.

Nia was already there, scrolling on an iPad.

"Hi," I said, putting my papers down at the head of the table.

"Mmmm," she said, distractedly.

Oh no. More hate mail?

"You okay?" I asked, taking a chair.

“They’re tenacious little bastards, these trolls,” she remarked. “That student keeps stoking the flames, and it gets them all riled up again.”

I wondered if she should be looking at it all, but I kept my opinions to myself. I’d been horribly cyber-attacked including online porn, so I was scarcely in a position to judge.

The students started filing in. When they’d settled down sufficiently, I began.

“Today I want to explore the question of whether white supremacists these days are making a concerted effort to construct an American civil religion of whiteness. Or, has American civil religion always been structured by whiteness and are they are merely drawing it out to its logical conclusion?

“President Biden was sworn in on a family bible that was more than a century old, in an inauguration ceremony full of religious symbolism. In his campaign, he had conjured American Civil Religion in its capacity to heal the nation and bring it together.

“By contrast, the violent mob that attacked the Capitol two weeks earlier had also used a plethora of religious symbolism, not as a source of reconciliation but as a source of division and intimidation. Crosses along with Viking symbols, neo-pagan imagery and fur-clad shamans all spoke to a post-Christian religious right. It was the uncivil version of civil religion.

“Civil Religion is the idea that American politics and identity are based on a religiously inspired but non-sectarian creed of common values and symbols. But as we dig deeper into what many would call ‘common values and symbols,’ we find the creed of ‘white is right’ not far below the surface.”

I knew this material so well, I hardly needed to consult my notes. I watched the students. About half were racial/ethnic minority, mostly African Americans. The rest were white. The students of color were intensely following my words, only making the occasional note. The white students wrote down nearly every word I said, heads bowed, shoulders hunched. Talk of white supremacy does really seem to embarrass many white people and cause them to retreat into themselves.

Well, I thought as I continued to speak, we’ll see how the discussion goes.

* * *

A chill wind from the west nearly blew my knit cap off as I made my way toward the building called, unimaginatively, "Central Administration." Beyond the Oxford style, medieval stone of the main quadrangle with its stained glass and turrets, Central Administration squatted at the far reach of the quad. It was a startling, Soviet-style rectangular block that had uniform, concrete walls, a flat roof, and square windows. The double-door in the front was grey. I could not imagine who had approved such architecture here. Even the next generation of this university's architecture, while whimsical, was not so inappropriate.

I checked the directory and took the elevator to the third floor. I'd been here before to the President's office at the top, during a cyberattack on me and a colleague. The president had decorated his concrete space with curved, art deco furniture. It too had been jarring.

I reached Ms. Sanchez's office, musing on how inappropriate decisions can be made in academia. The outer door was open, and I identified myself to the assistant sitting there.

"Go right in, Dr. Ginelli. Ms. Sanchez is expecting you," she said and gestured to the door opposite her desk. I knocked anyway and when a muted voice said, "Come in," I did.

Janice Sanchez rose from behind her desk and extended her hand. She was a slim, African American woman who had an athletic air, at least from what I could tell from her smooth movement standing up. She was wearing a grey and black weave tailored jacket over a grey silk blouse and slim, black pants. In my nursing bra, oversize jacket, and elastic waist pants, I felt a trifle dowdy.

I reached across her desk and shook her hand and then sat down in the chair she indicated.

"Thank you for seeing me," I said.

"Not at all," she replied. "What seems to be the problem?"

I explained as succinctly as I could how I was both a faculty member and a part-time consultant to the campus police.

"I have become concerned about the lack of progress on the investigation into the death of Coach Larsen at the aquatic center," I finished.

Ms. Sanchez folded her hands in front of her and bent her head, frowning. Then she looked up at me.

"You should know I had started to pursue getting Coach Larsen separated from this university," she said bluntly.

"My daughter Adrianna had just started practicing with the team, and I came by to watch a practice." She paused and then added, "I was a swimmer myself. What I saw was a man being overly friendly with the swimmers, calling them pet names, and even, at times, patting them and not just on the shoulder."

Her face became grim.

"I investigated his background, and he had, I guess I could say 'floated' around various swim teams on the southside of Chicago for quite a few years. For a time, he actually left coaching and worked in a sporting goods store. Then he was hired by another high school team and eventually he ended up here. I have been unable to find out exactly how that happened."

"If you, in your position, couldn't find that out, I consider that somewhat suspicious," I said slowly.

"Yes," she said firmly. "The problem, Dr. Ginelli, is getting reliable data from these other schools, or even from this school. If complaints are made, they are handled quietly, and the coaches just move on to another place. I started coming to the practices here just to monitor what was happening and perhaps identify students who might have a complaint to make."

She sighed deeply.

"My daughter was not happy with me for that," she said.

"I have reason to believe he was abusing young women on swim teams for a very long time. What that has to do with his death, however, is less clear," I said, gauging her reaction.

"Well, if by the end of this semester I had not been able to see him removed," she said in a clipped tone, "I was going to insist that Adrianna quit the team. She was also very unhappy with me about that."

She studied me for a moment.

"I can assure you I did not murder him, however," she said with only the hint of a smile. "If I thought he'd touched my daughter, well, that might have been another story."

"I know how you feel," I said. "I have five kids and if anyone touched one of them, I would hit them with a house at the very least."

"Yes," she said, a small smile emerging. "Where are those powers when we need them?"

"Will you still be coming to practices?" I asked as I rose.

"Yes, for a while, I think. I do not think the assistant coach knows anything about coaching swimming," she said as she rose too.

"Well, I may see you at the pool then," I said. "I have signed up to swim a couple of times a week."

She nodded.

"Thank you for your time," I said and departed.

Probably not the murderer, I thought as I trudged through the deepening December chill toward home. She had other ways to deal with Larsen. But she was certainly capable of it with that swimmer's strength she clearly still had.

18

~

Good therapists were those who really validated my experience.

— **Judith Lewis Herman**, *Trauma and Recovery*

"So, it's complicated," Tom said, coming out of the bathroom suite.

He was responding to my question about whether law enforcement could get access to Alice's therapist's records.

Of course, it is, I thought.

"Complicated how?" I asked.

"Well," Tom said, sitting down on the bed across from me, "You know HIPPA, right, the Health Insurance Portability and Accountability Act?"

I nodded.

"Well, it regulates the baseline medical privacy standards, but there are some exceptions. It's those exceptions that I hope Alice's lawyer is expert in since they could try to get a court order."

I groaned.

"But even if they don't do that, they still can have grounds for disclosure if it prevents harm. That's why they're raising the suicide issue. They may escalate, though, as HIPAA permits law enforcement to get a patient's records, including from a psychologist, if they claim they need to apprehend the perpetrator of a violent crime. That puts Alice in a very difficult position, it seems to me, given what you've said."

I was so frustrated I ground my teeth. Should I try to intervene in some way, or could I just make it worse? Worse, I told myself. I know the lawyer is really good. But the laziness of this so-called detective was really bothering me. They had latched on to the Black woman and didn't seem to feel they needed to look anywhere else.

Tom reached over and patted my shoulder.

"I know you feel you need to help Alice, but just don't take on too much, okay?"

"Don't push, Tom," I said with as calm a tone as I could manage. "I'm having a very hard time processing all that has happened on campus and with Alice."

"And your hormones," he began.

"Don't," I said, getting up to go get the girls for their last evening feeding.

It was too bad there was this tension between us, as the earlier part of the evening had gone very well.

Giles had cooked a Senegalese rice and meat dish that everyone loved. The girls had been in their bounce chairs at either end of the table, and Carol and Giles had stayed to eat with us. I would have invited Mrs. Brown to join us, but she'd told me earlier in the day she was meeting a friend for dinner in the neighborhood.

Kelly had been by in the late afternoon, and when she had smelled what Giles was cooking, she texted Zeke, and he had come by as well. Giles had started a second stewpot.

"So, Mom," Sam had asked after he had looked up from his plate for the first time after inhaling most of his stew, "when do they get to sit up in highchairs and have food?"

"They" was a frequent way the boys referred to Olivia and Natalie.

"A few more months, Sam," I said. "Olivia and Natalie need to be able to hold their heads up on their own and sit upright. But that's not all that long from now."

"Why are baby humans so helpless when they're born?" Mike asked.

"Well, their brains are smaller in order to fit through the birth canal," I said casually. The boys made faces at the mention of "birth canal."

"Yes," Tom added. "Human brains keep growing until they are 20 years old, in fact."

"My brain is still growing?" Sam said in shock.

"Well, I certainly hope so," Kelly chimed in.

"Yeah, well, I bet our brains will grow bigger than yours!" Mike snapped back.

The days of her calling them "dorks" and their calling her "Kelly smelly" were not that far behind us.

"Ha!" Kelly responded, but then Zeke chimed in.

"And the need to care for helpless babies has contributed to the creation of human communities and then civilization." He was a computer science major, but I knew from Kelly he also took a lot of psychology courses.

Olivia and Natalie started to fuss a little, perhaps tired of being talked about.

Carol and Kelly jumped up and each took one girl upstairs for a change. They were getting very good at it.

"Boys, let's clear and get the dishes into the dishwashers quickly, okay?" I said before they could leap up and go get out a game.

With two dishwashers, and I still marveled at that, we were quickly finished.

The boys and Tom headed for the family room along with Zeke. Giles lingered in the kitchen area.

"Carol, she loves *les enfants*," he commented in a quiet voice.

"I know Giles. Are you saying she wants to start trying for a baby?" I whispered back.

"I truly do not know, but I tell her it is good we get to practice now," he said softly as we could hear Carol and Kelly coming back down the stairs.

They carried the girls into the family room, strapped them in their bounce chairs, and Carol went back upstairs with Giles. Kelly and Zeke said they were taking off. Tom said he had to do evening rounds and headed for the garage.

Sam and Mike got out a deck of Uno and started laying out the game on the big coffee table.

"Mom, you playing?" Mike asked.

"Sure," I said, getting down on the floor. I was pretty sure I could get back up.

"Natalie's on my team," Mike said, gently moving her bounce chair closer to his side of the table.

"I got Olivia." Then he glanced at her. "You better wake up, Olivia. We gotta win," he joked.

Mike started the deal.

19

Third, the person [gains] authority over her memories; she can elect both to remember the trauma and to put memory aside.

—**Judith Herman**, *Trauma and Recovery*

SH: How are you sleeping these days?

AM: Well, I'm still slowed down by that medicine, but I do seem to sleep, and I don't dream. That's a blessing. Getting up is real hard.

SH: Are you ready to do some more work on the memories?

AM: I was thinkin' about that on the way over here. What are the worst ones? What ones do I wish I could just take a knife and cut out of my brain?

SH: What do you think now is what you'd call 'the worst one'?

AM: Well, I was always hurrying to get out of the locker room with all the other girls so I wouldn't be there alone, you know? But this one day, I forgot my house keys and my Mama worked, and I had to go back. I just had to go back. (Rapid breathing)

SH: Okay, do your breath work until you feel control coming back.

AM: (Breathing rapidly, then gradually in rhythm).

SH: That's very good.

AM: And he followed me. Must have. He backed me up against the lockers at the far end. Kept saying, "You want it. Tell me you want it." Over and over. (Breathing becomes very rapid).

SH: Okay, okay. Stop to get control.

AM: (Choked breaths in, then blown out)

SH: Take your time. We have nothing but time here. You are in control. You say when you are ready.

AM: (Breathing slowly) I wanted to scream NO! but I couldn't, I just froze like some stupid rabbit. I didn't say anything. I just stayed like that, frozen. Didn't say anything. Didn't say anything. Didn't say anything." (Sobs)

SH: And then what happened?

AM: I can't. I can't say it.

SH: (Reaching for a pad and pencil). Could you write it?

AM: I guess. (Reaches for the pad and, after a pause, writes.)

SH: (Reads).

AM: (Sobs).

SH: Can you say it now?

AM: (Hiccupping) Say what?

SH: Say the no. Say it loud.

AM: NO! NO! NO! No, you bastard. No! I don't want this. NO! (Breathing starts to return to normal).

SH: It wasn't your fault, you know, that you didn't say anything. He was wrong no matter what you did or didn't say. It's not your fault. It's not your fault. Say it with me.

AM/SH: It's not my fault. It's not my fault.

SH: It was never your fault.

20

Celebration is an active state, an act of expressing reverence or appreciation.

—Abraham Joshua Heschel

The end of the semester came roaring at us, the way it always did after Thanksgiving. Connecting with my class after teaching on the dreaded Zoom was better, but the students were leaning into the end of the term and not very engaged.

I kept up my swimming and would join Janice Sanchez on the bench by the side of the pool after I finished my laps. I wrapped myself in my big towel so as not to drip on her.

The first time I sat with her, I wanted to follow up with Katie Boen's suggestion that I talk to Paige Walsh, the senior transfer from Northwestern, and Alex Smith who was all state champion in Iowa. Janice pointed them out to me as they exited the pool.

"Do you think there's any point to my talking to the assistant coach?" I asked her as the pool area emptied out.

"I doubt it. She just strikes me as someone who buries her head in the sand. In HR, we are overseeing the search for a new coach, and I can tell you she won't be here much longer," Janice said, gathering her things and getting up, ready to leave. She looked down at me as I was still sitting, looking at the pool. "It's a tough time to recruit because the season will be underway soon. I may have to coach them myself for a while, and my daughter is livid about that."

Daughters, I thought as she said good-bye. My experience with Kelly was shorter but had been fraught with identity issues. All my friends with daughters despaired at one time or another, wondering if the conflict would ever stop.

I headed for the locker room to change and to speak to Paige and Alex.

They were willing to come talk with me at the coffee shop in the middle of campus in exchange for the promise of breakfast.

As they looked at the menus, I tried to size them up. They could have been sisters with their blond pixie cuts, broad shoulders, and tapered bodies. I wasn't going to get a pixie cut, but I hoped swimming would give my twin-stretched body some shape.

When our food came, I let them take a few bites and then asked them about the coach.

"Total creep," Paige said, pulling her croissant apart and feeding herself the pieces. "I mean, you could tell from the second he introduced himself by visually measuring your breasts he was one of those."

"One of what?" I asked, wanting her to be clearer.

"The swim coaches who try to get it on with the swimmers. The sport is full of them. Look what happened in California. And USA Swimming just kept covering up the complaints. Finally, they started publishing the names of coaches banned for sexual misconduct. You know, there's 191 names on that list now, and everybody knows it's the tip of the iceberg."

"Damn straight," Alex contributed around a mouthful of cinnamon bun.

I was startled they were so frank.

"Honestly," Paige continued, "we were trying to get some of the women on this team to report, but it's so uphill. They don't want the questions. And, I mean, who would?"

"Yeah," Alex said. "I mean Paige and I sized him up the first week, and we never left each other's side. Lots of the newbies have no idea, and I think he cornered a few. But would they tell us what he'd done to them? No way."

"Janice Sanchez wants to hire a new coach," I said, figuring I wasn't telling tales out of school.

"Yeah, Mrs. Sanchez is great. We ask her questions sometimes. She didn't make the Olympics, you know, but she was an alternate."

"No, I didn't know," I said, impressed all over again with Janice Sanchez.

"Do you know anyone who might have been mad enough to shove him in the pool, though?" I asked, looking at one then the other.

"Nah, I don't think so," said Paige.

"Lots of us knew he was on his way out," said Alex.

Katie hadn't, I thought. Or she knew and didn't tell me.

They picked up their backpacks and departed.

So, if the coach was about to be fired, to whom was he a threat? I asked myself as I walked back to the house.

When I got home, I called Mel and shared my thoughts.

"Right," he said, slowly. "Who wanted him dead?"

* * *

Tom and I had planned a holiday party at the last minute, and yet we'd had a lot of acceptances. We had asked our regular crew including Carol and Giles, Kelly and Zeke, Tom's brother Dave and our former wedding planner, now his girlfriend Victoria, my boss Adelaide, and my colleagues Hercules, Sandra, Nia, and Aduba and his family. Nia and Hercules both couldn't make it. They had family obligations out of town. And who could blame Nia for wanting to get out of town?

The biggest surprise was that Marco's parents, Natalie and Vince Ginelli, were coming all the way from their home in Wisconsin where Vince had been recuperating from a stroke he'd had in the spring. I had mentioned the party to Marco's parents when I called to check on them because they would have been hurt if I'd had a party, and they'd not been invited. Given the stroke, though, I thought they would decline. Not a chance. Marco's mother, Natalie, was jubilant about getting to see the twins and especially her namesake.

"Three days we come, Kri-s-tina!" Mama Ginelli chorused over the phone. She always seemed to think cell phones needed a boost in volume from her voice. "I make lasagna for party. You get *ingrediante*."

"O-kay," I said slowly, "but remember, no meat."

"*Si, lo so*," Natalie said impatiently and hung up.

I mentally added the ingredients for her lasagna to a shopping list and then thought it's a good thing we'd been able to turn the guest room back into a guest room.

The lasagna would not be enough, so I called my friends the African vegan caterers. I got in under the wire for such a large crowd.

I had also invited Mel and his family, but they were driving to Indiana and couldn't make it.

I never heard back from Alice.

* * *

The Ginellis arrived on a Friday. Natalie had phoned back to say Vince, Jr. was driving them. I was very relieved to hear that.

I was in our front bedroom when I heard the car pull up. I'd just finished feeding the girls.

The front door slammed open, and the boys were yelling "Nonna, Nonno!" or Grandma, Grandpa in Italian as they'd always called them. I could see they were running down the front walk. Molly was woofing a greeting.

I hurried down the stairs and through the open door. I could see the boys wrapped around Marco's parents. It brought a tear to my eye. I had considered them my parents for so many years, and I was touched they came. Of course, a granddaughter named for you would have drawn Natalie Ginelli to a space station if necessary.

Vince Jr. carried their bags into the front hall, gave me a quick "hiya," and started to head back to his car. I called after him asking him to stay for lunch, but he just waved a hand and drove away.

The boys had each hoisted one of the two bags and were already heading up the stairs. They constantly surprised me these days with how grown up they could suddenly be.

"Thanks, guys, for carrying the bags, but then you need to head to school," I called up the stairs. Since phys ed was their first period, I had agreed they could wait for their grandparents and take a late note to school.

"What would you like?" I asked, turning to Vince and Natalie.

"Like?" Vince chuckled, leaning only a little on his cane. "She wants to see those babies, Kristin."

So, we went up the stairs and headed down to the nursery. I walked behind Vince to be sure the stairs wouldn't be a problem. He was slow but steady.

The boys met us in the upper hall and followed us to the nursery.

I had alerted Mrs. Brown the Ginellis would be arriving and when she saw us in the doorway, she came over to greet them. I started to make introductions, but Natalie was heading to the bassinettes like she was pulled by a tractor beam.

"Look, look, Vince. They so perfect," she said, looking from one to another. Vince dutifully came over and glanced in each bassinette.

Sam and Mike followed them in.

"They're kinda small," Sam whispered, "but soon they'll get to sit up and eat regular food."

"And then they can play, too," Mike added.

Natalie turned to them, putting her arms around them. They were now as tall as she.

"Uncle Vince Jr. taught your dad so many things when your dad was small, and he was the older brother. You will do the same for the girls, no?"

"Yeah, yeah, we will," the boys mumbled, trying to hide their emotion.

I was less successful at hiding it. Tears rolled down my cheeks. My hormones were still out of whack, not that I'd tell Tom that.

"Well, yeah, we gotta go to school," Mike said, and they hurried away.

I gave Natalie a hug and then whispered, "Here's what I suggest. Rest in your room for a little while. I'll bring you some juice and snacks, and then when they wake up for the next feeding, Natalie, you can help me."

"*Si, si,*" she said abstractedly, turning again to look at the girls.

I let her enjoy it for a while, but I could see Vince was having trouble standing for so long, so I walked him over to the guest bedroom and then came back and detached Natalie from the babies and brought her too.

I left them moving their clothes into the armoire.

When I returned with the snacks, however, they were both sound asleep on the bed. I covered them with a light throw. I'd come back when the girls woke.

I was in my study room when Mrs. Brown came to get me. The girls were up and demanding to be fed.

Natalie was already in the nursery when I got upstairs.

"Vince, he sleep," she said softly. "I can help?"

"Yes," I said. "That would be great. This one is Natalie," I said, giving her namesake a pat. Baby Natalie was making quite a racket by now. "Pick her up, would you, and I'll get Olivia? I'll nurse Olivia, and you can give Natalie a bottle. How's that?"

"Oh, yes," she said, and I watched as the grown Natalie picked up baby Natalie with liver spotted hands made strong by decades of kneading dough.

"They have just been changed," Mrs. Brown contributed.

I went down to our bedroom and put Olivia on the bed. I got Natalie settled in a rocker and fixed a bottle with the device Tom had bought. Baby Natalie started sucking immediately and grown-up Natalie crooned an Italian lullaby to her.

I got started with Olivia who needed a little prodding at the breast. She didn't like to work as hard to get the milk, but she was learning.

Soon the room was filled with the soft sounds of babies eating and Natalie's lullabies.

* * *

"Hi!" Aduba's son Jachike, who liked to be called Jack, called when I opened the front door. "Sam and Mike said I could bring Hulk," he said, and I could see the tiny dog's head peeking out of his partially unbuttoned coat.

"Sure. That's fine, Jack. Take him in the family room next to the kitchen. Molly is already there," I said.

Then Sam and Mike came running down the hall yelling "Hi Jack," and they all departed.

This allowed Aduba and his wife Zala to actually enter the house.

"Welcome," I said as I took their coats. "So glad you could make it. There is juice, water, and tea in the front room along with some nibbles," I said quickly.

"Thank you so much," Zala said formally.

As they walked away, I could hear Zala softly ask Aduba something in what I thought was Yoruba.

"Small bites of food," he replied.

They were the last to arrive, and the room had already sorted itself out into discussion groups. Zala immediately headed to the sofa where Natalie and Victoria were deep in discussion. Zala was wearing a beautifully embroidered and sequined gown with batwing sleeves. Natalie and Zala had bonded before over embroidery at an earlier party, and I could see Natalie's tunic was heavily embroidered around the neck and sleeves, and Victoria's dress was a unique design of horizontal fabrics. I wondered if she'd made it herself.

She and Victoria greeted Zala, and the discussion barely paused.

Sandra was deep in conversation with Uncle Dave about environmental issues in Africa, it seemed, and Tom was listening in and nodding. Carol, Giles, Kelly, and Zeke were discussing some kind of issue on the campus. Adelaide was asking Vince for advice about cars.

All was well. I decided to check on the boys in the library. They had games, juice, and trays of finger food of their own in there.

"I really want a brother," Jack was saying. "I keep asking and asking. I mean, I have Hulk, but it's not the same." He made a move on what looked like a Monopoly board.

I heard a sigh and realized Aduba was behind me.

"It's okay," Sam said. "You can be our other brother. We can be like the Three Musketeers," and then he groaned as he landed in jail.

"Thanks!" Jack said.

"Yeah, right," Mike said. "You should come for a sleepover," he said as he collected rent from Jack who had just landed on one of his properties.

Aduba and I stepped away from the door.

"He does want a brother, but so far Allah has not blessed us," he said looking away.

"It's hard when that happens, Aduba," I said.

"Yes. Yes. It is very hard," he said, and he headed back to the living room.

I decided I'd check on the dogs before I followed him.

I pushed open the door into the kitchen/family room area, and I saw Molly stretched out on the floor by the fireplace. Hulk was sleeping in the middle of her big dog bed. Well, after all, I grinned to myself as I walked back to the front room, Hulk is a very big dog.

Kelly and I brought the girls down for a quick viewing by the others, and after the exclamations at their cuteness (totally deserved), we took them back upstairs.

As the evening wore down, I checked the buffet in the dining room. Of course, all the lasagna had been eaten. I'd learned, though, that African vegan food froze very well. We would need it over the holidays.

I shooed the Ginellis upstairs along with the boys. Natalie promised to "check on the babies" and Tom, Giles, Carol, Dave, Victoria, Kelly, Zeke and I made short work of helping the caterers clean up.

"A successful party," I said to Tom as we went upstairs to tuck the boys in.

"Yes, very," he said, "but I'm glad it ended early. I'm still beat."

"Me too," I said wearily.

But what I thought to myself was, I miss Alice.

21

Fourth, the memory of the traumatic event becomes a coherent narrative, linked with feeling.

— **Judith Lewis Herman**, *Trauma and Recovery*

SH: What would you like to talk about today?

AM: I'd like to talk about the evening I quit the team.

SH: Why is that important?

AM: It's when I decided to become a cop.

SH: Whenever you're ready.

AM: I was the last one out of the pool, but I wasn't worried because the other girls were still in the locker room. I was heading down the hall toward where they were, and he came out of a side office. I realized later he'd been waiting for me. I just stood there, frozen. And then, oh I can't say it. I've been silent about it so long. Can I have the pad again?

AM: (Writes, hands the pad back).

SH: (Reads).

AM: (Voice shaking). Then there were voices of girls coming back from the locker room, and he let me go. I ran into the locker room, picked up all my stuff. I didn't put on my dry clothes. I just grabbed it all and ran out toward the front door. (Pants)

SH: Keep breathing. Breathe through it.

AM: Yeah, okay. (Breathing) So, my mother was waiting, and I jumped in the car. She realized I was still in my wet suit with no shoes on, and it was winter, so she started yelling at me. I didn't say anything then. She cranked up the heater and drove home. I couldn't get warm even though I could feel the heat blasting out of the car vents. I was just so cold. When we got close to the house, I told her I was quitting the team and that I was going to become a cop.

SH: How did she respond?

AM: She was still angry about my getting the car seat wet and didn't seem to hear me. I ran in the house to my bedroom and locked the door. I ripped off my suit and threw it in the trash can in the bathroom. I put on lots of warm clothes, but I still couldn't warm up. Then my mother came and yelled through the door that I was getting my period. But I wasn't. And I never went near that pool complex ever again.

SH: And you went to the police academy after graduation?

AM: I did two years at the community college with courses I needed for the academy and then I went.

(Silence for a while)

AM: Here's what I want to ask you.

SH: Certainly.

AM: Why now? Why this freezing panic nonsense now?

SH: I've told you, it's not nonsense. It's a defense mechanism we have along with flight or fight. When your brain concludes you can't do anything, you freeze, in the hope that the predator will overlook you or not be interested any more or at least that it will be over more quickly. And I think you know why now.

AM: Because I saw him dead, and I'd wished it so much. And it brought it all back.

SH: Exactly.

AM: That's what I thought.

SH: How are you doing on the quarter dose of the anti-depressant?

AM: I'm feeling better in general. Not much appetite, but not bad.

SH: I think you can stop that now completely, and we'll check in at your next appointment.

AM: Thanks, and Merry Christmas and happy Kwanzaa.

SH: The same to you.

22

There is nothing more deceptive than an obvious fact.

—**Sir Arthur Conan Doyle**, *The Bascombe Valley Mystery*

The Christmas break week had been hectic. Vince Jr. had picked up the Ginellis two days after the party. Nonna was tearful leaving the twins, and there were many assurances of visits in the future. Mrs. Brown had gone to be with her family for the holidays, Giles and Carol had flown to Maine to visit her family, Victoria and Uncle Dave had gone away together to Utah for a ski vacation, and Zeke and Kelly had gone with Zeke's family to their cottage in Michigan and were cross-country skiing. Tom had some scheduled time off from the hospital, but he'd had a few emergencies.

The boys had really stepped up. When Tom was at the hospital, I'd asked one and then the other to give a bottle, and I think my needing them for that helped them grow even more into the big brother role. Fortunately, the girls were sleeping as much as 4 ½ to 5 hours a night, so Tom and I were not as exhausted as we'd been when we'd had the newborns to manage ourselves.

I will say take-out food became the norm. The Uber-Eats driver and I were now on a first-name basis.

So, I almost broke into song when Mrs. Brown, Carol and Giles came back. "Look how much they've grown!" was the general consensus.

I thought the boys needed a big thank you for stepping up, and Tom and I decided to take them to Disney World for spring break. The new Marvel characters exhibit was much coveted by the kids and their friends.

What I really needed to focus on was who had killed Coach Larsen. I wasn't teaching my own course in the January term. I only had to repeat the lectures for Nia's class that I'd done in the spring. There had been so much demand for her class after the cyberbullying that she'd agreed to offer it again in a one-week intensive format in what was called J-term.

During the Christmas break, while my body had been busy feeding the girls, doing laundry, ordering take-out food and groceries, my mind had not left the conversations I'd had with the swim team members Paige and Alex and then with Mel. It was clear Mel's question, "Who wanted him dead?" was key. Once Mel had ruled out the grieving father of the young woman who'd committed suicide, he'd had an iron-clad alibi, who was left?

The holidays seemed to have slowed down the police investigation, what there was of it, but I had heard from Anna on Thursday of break week that Alice's lawyer was going to court to prevent that detective from getting access to Alice's records with the therapist. Anna thought he could delay that, but it was clear they had no suspects other than Alice, and they could possibly succeed in getting her records.

My first full day of a regular schedule, therefore, I devoted to researching who might have wanted that swim coach dead.

* * *

Paige had said "look what happened in California" so I thought I'd start there. I googled "swimming sex abuse cases in California" and was inundated with information. A news article from mid 2020 was headlined "Six Women File Lawsuits Against USA Swimming Over Alleged Sexual Abuse by Coaches."

The suits the women filed alleged the national governing body had failed to protect them against abuse by coaches creating a "culture of abuse" that exposed dozens of underage swimmers to abuse and harassment. Swimmers would file complaints only to have them go nowhere and the coach moved to a different team.

The article quoted one of the former swimmers who was suing.

"USA Swimming enabled Mitch Ivey to abuse me and as a result, I've suffered from years of depression, low self-esteem, and panic attacks on top of acute anxiety. I still suffer from the trauma today that will stay with me for the rest of my life. USA Swimming must clean house and get rid of the coaches and executives that created this culture that condoned sexual abuse by coaches."

It was chillingly similar to what I guessed was the case for Alice.

I read further and noted that these lawsuits had been made possible because California had passed a new law that allowed sex abuse victims to confront not only their abusers but also the organizations that had protected them. There was a three-year window to file past claims that had expired under the old statute of limitations.

My milk addled brain groped for something I might have read recently about Illinois.

I bookmarked the 2020 article and googled "new Illinois law allows lawsuits against sexual predators" and came up with another slew of articles.

Bingo. Just 8 months ago, Illinois had passed a law modeled on the one in California.

Could this be what was new and put Coach Larsen in the crosshairs? Who besides Larsen would be threatened by this window to file civil lawsuits over not only abuse by coaches but also those who ignored the complaints and covered it up?

I needed to call Anna, my lawyer, friend, and giver-of-dark-chocolate-truffles.

Just then Mrs. Brown came in and let me know the girls were clamoring to be fed.

I took my phone and went upstairs to nurse them in our bedroom and call Anna.

As soon as I got settled with the girls and my nursing pillow, I used the voice feature to call Anna. I did not expect to get right through to her, but she picked up. I could hear road noise in the background. She was in one of her limos, I guessed.

After a few pleasantries and promises by Anna to drop by again, I got down to my question.

Since I didn't need to explain the situation with Alice, I asked about this new law.

"Yes, it's wise to confront the inadequacy of these statutes of limitation. Given how long it can take for those who have been abused to recover enough to report, the statutes of limitation effectively keep essential legal action from happening," she said, and I could hear her nails tapping, likely on the armrest.

I thought about Bill Cosby and all those he'd abused. Those women had been unable to get justice because the incidents were so far in the past.

"So, Anna, is the law in Illinois the same as in California? Can organizations that covered up reports of abuse also be held liable?"

"Yes. In fact, I'd say the Illinois law is slightly stronger in that area. Our firm is handling several cases that are moving forward. The three-year window is narrow and getting documentation, what there is of it, can take time. But they are moving."

This, I thought. This is what is new.

"Do you know of any cases involving Coach Larsen, the swim coach who was drowned at the university?" I asked her.

"No, I don't, but I can ask around."

"Thanks, Anna," I said and hung up.

Natalie had already finished.

23

Fifth, the person's damaged self-esteem has been restored. Sixth, the person's important relationships have been reestablished.

— **Judith Lewis Herman**, *Trauma and Recovery*

SH: So, when do you start back to work?

AM: Tomorrow.

SH: How are you feeling about that?

AM: Well, Jim is glad. I think he's less worried about me, but he's been fretting, I know that. And Shawna is better. She's liked having me around more.

SH: Yes, but how are you feeling?

AM: (Wrings hands) There's a couple of nerves I wish would calm down. I don't really think I'll turn into some freezing statue if I see something that reminds me. (Chuckle) Unless one of the educated idiots starts trying to swim in the snow on the campus.

(Long pause)

SH: But you think you're doing okay now that you're off the anti-depressants?

AM: I guess so.

SH: What do you think you can do if you do feel yourself start to freeze?

AM: Breathing. Yeah, yeah. I know.

(Pause)

SH: The breathing is good. What else works for you these days?

(Silence)

AM: I can call you.

SH: You have my cell number if you have a problem, correct?

AM: Yes.

SH: Suppose you can't reach me?

AM: I leave you a message, talk as long as I want.

SH: Right. Breathing and also just saying out loud what's bothering you can help you prevent freezing. What else?

AM: Taking positive action. I know, I know. I read that stuff you gave me.

SH: Positive action like what?

AM: I don't want some other young girl to end up feeling like this. That's for damn sure. So, I guess tryin' to get a decent coach for the university. That would be positive.

SH: It would.

AM: So, we done?

SH: Do you feel done?

(Silence)

AM: No. I'm still afraid I'll freeze at some stupid moment.

SH: Then we'll meet again, let's say in three weeks?

AM: Yeah, okay, but I'll call if I start feeling a freeze comin' on.

(Chuckle)

SH: What are you laughing about?

AM: That *Frozen* movie Shawna and her friends like so much. I've heard that song "Let it go" so much I can sing it in my sleep. I was wondering just now if the grownup who wrote that felt some freezing coming on and wanted to let it go.

SH: Could be. Lots of people have been traumatized.

AM: You got that right.

24

~

If you're going through hell, keep going.

—Winston Churchill

Mel had texted me and asked if we could meet at the campus police station in the mid-morning. I'd texted back that I could and headed over there after swimming my laps and taking a boilingly hot shower.

Invigorated from the swimming and warmed up from the shower, I bundled myself into a new coat Tom had gotten me for Christmas that made me look like a bright red Michelin man. It was full length and incredibly warm. I'd tried it on right after I'd opened the box and had immediately begun sweating. Tom had also given me a cobalt blue, long, knitted scarf and matching knit hat with a visor that could be pulled down over the top half of the face to block icy Chicago winds. When I put all these items on, I felt impervious to Chicago weather.

I crossed the campus in the direction of the campus police station. It always made me smile how schizophrenic it was. The outside was a charming, three story, red brick building covered in ivy that had been a private school in the last century. Inside, however, it was just as rundown, badly lit, and full of various smells best not identified as any downtown police station. The worn linoleum could have been transported from Branch 36 out California Avenue, the cop shop I used to work out of when I was a Chicago police detective.

The outside reassured the campus that the police fit right in, and the inside told possible perpetrators, "We mean business."

I took off my long scarf, pulled off my hat and unbuttoned the coat as soon as I got into the lobby. The drawback of this cocoon of warmth was the sweating profusely upon entering a building.

I headed up the stairs toward the office that Mel used when he was in the building. By the top of the stairs, I had shrugged off the coat and draped it over my arm.

I knocked and Mel called, "Come in." I opened the door and found him sitting at the small table that was near the window. And sitting next to him was Alice Matthews.

"Alice!" I cried out and dashed over to pull her into a hug.

"Okay, okay, simmer down," she said, drawing back in her chair. "I'm here, I'm working, let's get started."

I stood and looked down at her, smiling at her typical grumpy response.

"Quit it, will you?" she said, but she couldn't keep a little smile from curving her lips.

"Alright, but you're here, and I'm glad to see you," I said dumping my coat, scarf, and hat on one of the chairs and taking the other.

I kept the smile in place, but she didn't look good. Far from it. She must have lost ten pounds or more since I'd seen her, and her face was drawn, lines I'd never seen before running down from her nose to the corners of her mouth.

"Look," Mel said, "glad you are happy to see each other but let's get started. We have a lot to cover. Kristin, why don't you summarize what you've found out from the swimmers on the team, that one mother of a team member and then I'll go over getting together with the father on the girl who committed suicide."

I was all for that plan, but I saw Mel was radiating tension in his neck and shoulders and covering it with being all business.

I started with exploring the swim facility and finding out that one 8-pound hand weight was missing.

Mel broke in.

"I searched that whole area behind the swim building, but I didn't find it," he said flatly.

"Well, I don't know if the Chicago cops even searched there. Alice, did any of the cops who've interviewed you ask about a weight?

Alice was stone-faced, and my heart skipped a beat. For a moment, I feared she might slide into that freezing thing she did, but she only took a few deep breaths and replied calmly, "No."

I went on to Kelly connecting me to Katie Boen, and then Katie telling me about Paige and Alex. And Adrianna and her mother who worked in HR who had been an alternate on the US Olympic swim team.

"No kidding," Mel said.

"Yeah. And she's helping out until they can hire a decent coach," I said.

Alice looked very grim.

I was on the fence about bringing up the scandal in California and the new law here in Illinois with the three-year window for reporting.

I was saved from having to decide that when the phone rang on the desk. Mel got up to answer it.

"Yes, Captain," he said. Then he looked over at Alice and put his finger to his lips.

"That detective is here, Booth? No, I haven't seen Alice Matthews today. Yeah, yeah. I'll tell her to come to your office when I see her, but I frankly don't know her schedule."

He hung up.

"Alice, you need to get out of here," Mel said. "That detective is here with two other cops. You need to get with your lawyer pronto."

Alice looked stunned.

"Look, Alice. Put on my coat, scarf and hat and go out the back way. Call your lawyer when you're clear of the building."

Alice shook herself.

"There's no way I'm passin' for a 6-foot white woman," she said irritably.

"You don't have to be me," I said sharply. "You just have to not be you!" And I picked up my coat and held it out so she'd put it on.

She sighed but did it.

I handed her the hat and scarf and dug around in my purse while she did that. I located my sunglasses and handed them to her. She took them and held them. Then she put them on and picked up her purse.

"Go!" Mel said and went to the door. He opened it and checked down the hall both ways.

"Clear. Get out the back. Call the lawyer. Kristin's right."

Alice headed out the door.

Mel shut it and turned toward me.

"This smells like a trap," he said angrily.

"I think so too. Gutierrez must have told that detective she'd be off medical leave today, and they came to get her, shutting out her lawyer."

"Right. Well, let's sit still for a while. I think we'll get a visit in a few minutes."

Sure enough, there was a knock on the door.

Just then I spotted Alice's peacoat hanging on a hook on the wall. I grabbed it and pulled out a filing cabinet drawer that I knew usually contained bags of cookies. I took out the cookies and stuffed the coat in.

I put the bags of cookies on top of the filing cabinet and whirled toward the table.

Just in time as the door opened with no more knocking, and Captain Gutierrez and a fiftyish, grey-haired man in a well-tailored, grey suit came in. The suited guy's face was slightly grey as well. In fact, he did not look well.

"Not here yet?" Gutierrez said, looking around.

Well, unless Alice was hiding under the cookies, it was obvious she wasn't here.

I held out my hand to the newcomer.

"I'm Dr. Kristin Ginelli of the Philosophy and Religion Department. I consult part-time for the campus police. I used to be a detective out of Branch 36," I said.

"Booth," the largely grey man said.

Then he paused.

"Ginelli. Were you related to Marco Ginelli? I knew him," he said quietly.

"Yes," I said, the familiar stab piercing my heart. "I'm his widow."

"How do you do?" he said formally, shaking my hand.

Not very well right now, I thought.

Captain Gutierrez looked steadily at Mel but didn't say anything. Detective Booth looked decidedly suspicious.

"Well, we'll have to find another way to contact Mrs. Matthews," he said slowly, not giving Alice the dignity of her police title.

Captain Gutierrez held the door for him, and they left.

My phone vibrated in my purse.

"Coffee shop" was all it said.

"Alice?" Mel asked.

"Yeah. She's in the coffee shop. I'll go meet her. But listen Mel, I think this new Illinois law could be the trigger for why this abusive coach was murdered. I think we should follow up on who was supervising him when he coached on the southside. Those articles I sent you show that the supervisors who looked the other way got into a lot of trouble."

"I totally agree," Mel said. "While you go meet Alice, let me get his employment history from Mrs. Sanchez and research that."

"Great," I said and for a moment looked around for my coat. Then I realized it was on Alice.

I pulled out the filing cabinet door and got out her peacoat. It smelled like chocolate chips. I turned it inside out and shrugged it on. It was an extremely tight fit and much too short.

Mel looked at me.

"You better go out the back way too. It's obvious that's not your coat."

"Yep," I said and grabbed my purse. I texted Alice "on my way" and trotted out the back.

* * *

Alice was sitting at an outside table in the only shaft of sunlight left in Chicago. She had a cardboard cup of tea and had gotten a cup for me.

She didn't even smile when she saw me sausaged into her peacoat.

Silently we exchanged coats.

"So, what did the lawyer say?" I asked when I took a sip of the hot drink. It was just decaf, I could tell.

"Yeah, he thinks it was a trap, and he is pissed. I like that about him. He gets good and mad when they're playin' games. So, I'm gonna drive down and meet him at his office in an hour. He'll call that Booth and say I heard he was lookin' for me. We'll go together to meet him if that detective still wants to see me. Lawyer thinks since I've been seeing a therapist, the detective thinks he can rattle me good, make me confess, I don't know, to shooting Tupac or some damn crime or other."

I thought they'd just arrested a guy for shooting Tupac, but I kept my mouth shut.

"Well, Alice, I think the line we need to follow is why was that coach killed now. I have some ideas on that. Later in the week you and Mel and I can meet again, go over that."

I watched her over the rim of my coffee cup.

"Yeah. Okay. Good of you to do this, Kristin," she said in a horribly subdued voice.

This was not good.

"Well, you know me, Saint Ginelli," I said in a deliberately sarcastic voice.

Alice gave a small snort. I was so glad to hear it.

"I know, I know. You just like stickin' your nose in things," she said. The words were right, but the tone was so low energy.

"Can't help it," I bantered back. "Listen, I have to go give a lecture. Call me after you and the lawyer meet with that detective.

She just nodded, got up and walked away. She left her remaining tea behind.

* * *

I walked home and nursed the girls while I drank my shake. The lecture was not until 1, so I had time to rest and think a little. Nursing was very good for that.

Alice was still not one hundred percent, that was for sure. And why would she be? These things take time to get over, I knew. The trauma of Marco's murder had taken me years to get over. Of course, I'd not gotten therapy like Alice had. I knew it could make a difference.

I carried the sleeping babies back to the nursery and chatted with Mrs. Brown a little. Mostly about their poop. Motherhood or childcare is not for the squeamish.

I walked back to campus and up the stairs. This was good exercise too. I hung my big puffer coat up on a hook on my side of the office, and it immediately pulled the hook off of the wall. Well, I'd need to get a hammer and nail, I thought and just dumped everything on my chair.

My notes were already printed out and on my desk. I picked up the folder and headed down to the classroom.

Nia was already there with several of the students who had signed up for this intensive, and they were talking about the final assignment.

Finally, the rest of the class trickled in, and I had managed to say, "The 19th century social reformers" when Adelaide rushed into the room.

"There's been a bomb threat on this building. Everyone out. Now!"

She went across the hall to knock on Aduba's office door. Nia, the class, and I sprinted for the door.

Sandra hadn't been in our office a few minutes ago, but I opened the door to check and to get my new coat. I was damned if I'd let a bomber blow up my Christmas present.

Then I sprinted behind everyone else and made it outside to the quad where 6 police cars and 7 or 8 campus police were drawn up. Assorted bystanders were asking "What's happening?"

Crime scene tape was being strung between trees and trashcans to keep people back.

Just then a blue and white truck raced over the grass and pulled up directly in front of the building.

Out of the back, the doors opened and a German shepherd and a guy in one of those dark-green, bomb disposal suits got out.

The giant suit put my puffy coat to shame. The dog looked impatient to get started.

I dearly hoped they wouldn't find anything. The dog had no bomb coat.

I spotted Adelaide further back in the crowd. She had come out without her coat and was shivering and looked shocked. I pulled off my big scarf and wrapped it around her. Then I opened my coat and stood behind her, placing myself between her and the biting, west wind.

"Thanks," she said, starting to shake a little less.

"They won't find anything, Adelaide," I said. "This is just an escalation of the cyberbullying. But you know what's good news?"

She turned her head to look at me.

"What could possibly be good news about this?"

"The cyberbullying just became a federal crime. The university can't hide behind their BS policy anymore."

"Okay," Adelaide said slowly. "That is good news."

I knew two FBI guys in the Chicago office who were very good. I started making plans to call them tonight.

But first I needed to call Tom.

25

Life has many ways of testing a person's will, either by having nothing happen at all or by having everything happen all at once.

- Paulo Coelho

"Mom! Mom!" I could hear the yelling and the backpacks hitting the floor from the back of the house.

"Yes!" I called. "I'm here. What's wrong?"

The thunder of four feet and four paws told me they were running down the central hall of the house, closely followed by Molly who always managed to be in the front hall at exactly the time the boys were expected home.

"Mom!" Sam said breathlessly when they saw me. "There was a bomb, at the university!"

"Did you know?" Mike queried, staring at me.

"It was a bomb scare, not a bomb," I said in a quiet voice. "And yes, I knew someone had called and said there was a bomb. But they were lying."

They stared at me, processing that. Apparently, the word "bomb" had made its way through the lower school with the speed of sound.

"But that's still a crime, right?" Mike wanted to know, now heading toward the new refrigerator, Sam on his heels.

"Oh yes, it's a crime alright to make a bomb threat. People can go to prison for years for doing that."

"Can we have ice cream?" Mike said, now peering into the freezer.

Leave it to Mike to try to parlay a bomb scare into an afterschool special treat.

"Let's save that for dessert tonight and have apples and yogurt with some of Carol's parents' maple syrup."

"Yeah, well the syrup is good," Sam acknowledged.

Carol was trailing in now, and she smiled.

Snacks were fixed, and the boys queried me more about the bomb threat.

"So did you ever have to look for a bomb, Mom, like when you were a cop?" Mike asked.

"No, they have specially trained people for that. Like today, a truck came up and a man in a big, puffy suit and a helmet got out with a dog and checked the building. Then they signaled all clear."

"Wow. And you saw that?" Sam exclaimed, and then shoveled in some yogurt.

"I did. Lots of people did," I said, trying again for a calm tone. I did not want to tell them it had been my office building.

"Was the dog wearing one of those bomb suits?" Sam asked.

"No, I don't think they make them for dogs," I said.

"Well, that stinks," Sam said.

"I wonder how they train dogs to sniff bombs," Mike said, gazing down at Molly who was blatantly begging for their snack.

"Maybe by putting maple syrup on them?" Sam joked.

We all chuckled, though Carol's and my eyes met over the top of the kids' heads.

She knows it was my building, I thought.

* * *

After the boys had gone to bed, Tom, Carol, Giles, Mrs. Brown, and I met in the library with the door shut. Mrs. Brown had been a little puzzled by being asked to join the family meeting, but I explained it involved her too. She arrived carrying the baby monitor.

"What else have you heard, Kristin?" Tom asked, his anxiety pretty well masked except for a vein in his forehead that was throbbing.

"The threat was phoned in at exactly 1 pm and specifically mentioned that there was a bomb in the classroom where, and I quote, 'that white-hating N-word teaches.'"

Mrs. Brown looked stunned.

I explained briefly about Dr. Turner's class and the cyberbullying.

"Well, that's awful," she said, her eyes wide behind her sequin-trimmed glasses.

"It is indeed," I commented.

Carol looked horrified, but Giles sighed more with a tone of grief than anything else.

"So, what do you think that means for our safety here?" Tom asked, his voice now as tense as his forehead.

"Well, we already have very good security in place," I said, trying for the same quiet tone I'd used with the boys. I actually wanted to scream my frustration at how much havoc these haters were causing.

"We have the bars on the lower windows, the window and door alarms, the front and back steel doors, and the security cameras with record function. What we don't do, however, is alarm the house each time we enter and leave, and I think we need to start doing that."

I had arranged a serious security upgrade to our house the previous year when we'd had hate crimes by white supremacists on campus, though no bomb threats.

"I think I'll get that security company that did the upgrade out here again and tie those keypad door locks to the security codes. Make it simpler for the boys. For all of us, really. We don't want to keep punching a dozen buttons when we come and go."

Carol, Giles, and Mrs. Brown nodded, but Tom sat and looked at me without saying anything for a whole minute.

"Tom, do you have anything to add?" I finally asked.

"No," he said slowly, "though a bomb can be left on the front or back porch without someone having to disarm the system."

"True," I said. "But remember there was no actual bomb. Most of the time these threats are exactly that, threats. Some wacko with his or her cellphone."

"Most of the time is not all," Tom said firmly.

"No," I acknowledged. "It's not."

"I'll call the security company tomorrow," I said, and we all rose.

As I followed Tom up the stairs, I could see the tension in his shoulders. Surgery required managing risk, but this kind of risk was very difficult to manage.

My cell phone signaled a new text.

Emergency faculty meeting tomorrow 8 am. Dr. Winters

* * *

I walked toward campus wearing my big puffer coat. It was 12 degrees out with a strong, west wind. I'd lectured the boys about keeping their hats and gloves on until they got inside the school.

The text tone sounded again.

Coffee this am? Alice

I was so glad to see that. I texted back.

I can do 10 or later.

10 fine, she replied.

I took off my coat before walking up the stairs. No point in dying of heatstroke. I scanned my keycard and dumped my outside clothes in my chair. The hook was still lying on my desk instead of up on the wall. Sandra's desk was empty. She must already be at the meeting.

Grabbing my half caff coffee, I pushed open the door and entered. Captain Gutierrez was at the head of the table, Adelaide next to him on one side, Aduba on the other, then Sandra, and across from her, Nia. Down the center of the table, a computer was open, and I could see the flicker of the screen from the side. I bet Donald was attending by Zoom, the coward.

I nodded at the room and sat just across from virtual Donald.

"Good," Adelaide said firmly. "Welcome again, Captain Gutierrez. What do you have to tell us?"

"The call making the bomb threat was at 1 pm and from a burner phone. The caller referenced a phrase used by that student blogger who has been stirring people up, and the FBI will be speaking to that person later today. It is likely the person who made the bomb threat is one of his, I guess you would say, followers."

So much for 'free inquiry' I thought.

"Will that student now be expelled?" Nia asked.

"I do not know," the captain said, his mustache bristling. He was irritated because he was being kept out of the loop, I thought. "But I do know the administration is meeting on that issue right now."

"I should have been informed about that meeting," Nia said irritably. "Please excuse me. I need to call my lawyer."

She left briskly.

"Any questions?" Captain Gutierrez asked.

"Can Dr. Turner's class be moved to another building?" a voice asked from the computer.

"That is not my area," Gutierrez said shortly.

Adelaide frowned at the computer but did not comment.

"Then, I will keep your department chair posted," Gutierrez said, and he too departed at speed.

I think I'll call my FBI contacts Paul Lindsay and Kamal Nadar, I thought as I headed back to my office.

* * *

I left a message for both Lindsay and Nadar. I knew them to be reasonably trustworthy in that "I don't tell civilians anything" sort of way they had. Nadar did cybercrimes, so I guessed he'd be in on the blogger/bomb threat angle, but who knew?

At 9:45 I headed over to meet Alice. It felt like old times, us meeting for coffee.

I saw her from a distance. She was sitting outside at a small café table even though the temperature had not yet gotten above 20 degrees. Two cardboard cups were sitting in the middle of the table, and I was surprised the steam coming off them didn't immediately turn to snow.

"Hey Alice," I said, sitting down. "What's up?"

She looked up at me and narrowed her eyes.

"You mean besides a murder and a bomb threat?"

Ah, sarcasm. Music to my ears.

"No. That's plenty actually," I said, taking the cup closer to me and sipping it. Totally decaf. Alice was trying to get me off caffeine again. I sniffed lightly and couldn't smell any cigarettes on her, though since my nose was slightly frozen it wasn't a true test.

"The lawyer made short work of that Booth, I'll tell you that," Alice said, pulling her own cup toward her. "He made an appointment, told them 'such tactics will not be tolerated, and I will go to Judge Somebody or Other if you persist.'"

Alice actually smiled.

"That cop, he's almost afraid of the lawyer, you know? I'm trembling in my boots, but nothin' bad has happened to me so far."

"Good," I said quietly, "but we need to end this, Alice. Get the right person in custody."

"Yeah. I know." She took a drink of her tea. "I do think that coach was bouncing around from one team to another even after he, you know, coached my team. Had to be protected by someone." She swallowed hard, then took a sip of tea again.

"Right. So, I've been doing some research," I said, and I rooted around in my purse.

"Course you have," Alice said dryly. "What else is new?"

I took some papers out and spread them on the ice-cold table.

"The local association of USA Swimming that your team was in had the same guy on the executive committee for basically all the years Larsen was coaching on the southside. And," I paused for effect, "he's currently running for congress from that same district. How's that for motive? You combine that with the new law here in Illinois on a reporting window, and that guy's political career would be toast if it came out that he'd been passing Larsen on from one team to another despite complaints."

Alice took the papers. I hated to see that her hands shook despite her gloves, but she read them thoroughly. I finished my lukewarm, terrible decaf and waited.

"It's motive," she said flatly.

"You bet. And I'm going to visit his campaign headquarters tomorrow," I said. "I have an appointment. You know, I may even volunteer," I said with a grim smile.

"You would, wouldn't you?" Alice said, her voice catching.

"Yeah, well I would," I said trying not to choke up myself.

"I'll let you and Mel know what I find out," I said getting up and taking our empty cups to toss in the recycling.

"Kristin," Alice said slowly.

"No, Alice. Forget it."

"I can't," she said quietly. "Not yet."

* * *

I hurried home because I had an appointment with the security guy who would do the keypad conversion for us.

He was already parked in front of our house.

I briefly told him what I needed, and he and a guy I didn't recognize got out some tools from the back of their van. Good, they could work on it today.

I raced upstairs where I could hear the girls starting to kick up a ruckus.

Mrs. Brown was changing Olivia while Natalie yelled at the top of her tiny lungs.

"She's changed already," Mrs. Brown said. "I'll bring Olivia in a minute."

I picked up Natalie and hustled down to our bedroom and got settled in the rocker with the double nursing pillow.

My milk was slow to let down, and that set them both off. I'm racing around too much, I thought and tried to settle myself. Natalie got herself going finally, but Olivia took longer. Finally, the little mouths tugging did the job.

I was just getting into a milk coma when my cell phone rang. It was on the stool in front of me, and I could see it was Rev. Jane Miller Gershman, the campus chaplain. She and I had become friends, and she had performed Tom's and my wedding service.

I was able to hit the button for speaker, and Jane's soft voice came on.

"Hello, Kristin. I hope this is not a bad time," she said.

Well, I thought, there are better times, but I just said, "No, go ahead."

"I wanted to talk to you about the girls' baptisms," she said.

No, I thought. Not one more thing. I actually cannot take one more thing.

"I'll have to get back to you on that, Jane," I said in as nice a voice as I could.

"Well, okay," she said, "but there is a time coming up that . . ."

I cut her off. I had to.

"Jane, I honestly cannot talk about this right now," and I hung up.

26

You know my methods, Watson. There was not one of them which I did not apply to the inquiry. And it ended by my discovering traces, but very different ones from those which I had expected.

—**Sir Arthur Conan Doyle**, *The Adventure of the Crooked Man*

The next morning after Tom, the boys, Carol, and Giles had left, I put the girls in their bounce chairs downstairs and read aloud to them. Molly lay between them, I thought at first to watch over them, except she fell asleep almost immediately.

After two recitals of *Goodnight Moon*, a book I had long ago memorized, they went to sleep as well, and I carried them upstairs to Mrs. Brown.

I went to my home office and sent Jane an email apologizing for being abrupt on the phone. I said I had a lot on my plate and would get back to her about the baptism. That would hold her off for a while, but at the rate problems were piling up in my life, the girls would be in Middle School before I got around to planning a baptism.

I googled Steven William Cook, "call me Steve," the middle-aged white lawyer who had been on the local USA Swimming Association Council in her area since Alice had been a teenager.

Cook was campaigning in the 2nd congressional district, on the Chicago south-east side, to be the Democratic nominee for election to

Congress. Beverly Hopkins, the African American woman who had served the district for two decades, was retiring.

I clicked on his campaign website and brought up his bio. Sure enough, his time on the association swimming council was listed under "Accomplishments."

I clicked on websites about the 2nd congressional race and saw Cook was scarcely the only person competing to be the nominee and effectively the congressperson. No Democrat had lost in that district in decades, but they had been, in the main, African American. I wondered what Steve as a white guy thought he could do to secure the nomination.

I went back to Steve's website and soon enough I saw his pitch. "Jobs! Jobs! Jobs!" was the main heading. "Call me Steve" was touting his ability to bring jobs to the southside devasted by the collapse of the steel industry that had fueled the economy of that area for so long. I scrolled down to see if I could find what kinds of jobs he was promising, and there was, unsurprisingly, very little detail. There was a picture of workers in a warehouse, though. There were lots of abandoned steel mills in the 2nd congressional district. I bet they would be perfect for lots of Amazon warehouses or server farms. Not exactly high-paying jobs.

I wondered who was funding Steve's campaign so far.

I dialed the number for the campaign office and got a recording of the candidate's voice welcoming me and asking me to leave my name and contact information. I did so. I went upstairs to change out of mommy clothes, and my cell rang.

"Ms. Ginelli?" a pleasant, male, sightly southern accent asked me.

"Why yes," I said softly, my suburban, white woman identity firmly in place.

"This is Chris Bentley. I'm the campaign manager for Steve Cook, and I got your message inquiring about his candidacy. Do you live in the district?"

I'd prepared for this.

"Not yet," I said, "but we are looking at a home in Olympia Fields, and I wanted to get a sense of Mr. Cook's positions as they might affect the area."

Olympia Fields was comparatively white and affluent compared to the other towns in the 2nd.

"Well, now, that's what Ah call doing your homework," Bentley chuckled.

"I always do," I said truthfully.

"Can you get here today, perhaps around 1 pm? You can meet the candidate. He is planning to be in the office this afternoon."

"I think I can manage that." I chuckled. "That is, if the Dan Ryan cooperates."

"Surely true," Bentley replied and dictated the address to me.

"Drive safely," he said.

* * *

I drove slowly along the Dan Ryan, the only speed possible on the frequently jammed highway that ran north/south on Chicago's near west side. The east side was a giant lake, and I was disinclined to take a boat, though at this point rowing might have been faster.

I'd fed the girls and checked in with Mrs. Brown for a few minutes about giving them some tummy time when they woke up. Mrs. Brown knew her stuff, and we discussed how long the tummy time should be.

Cook's campaign headquarters was in Matteson whose motto was "A Home for Business, A Heart for Family." I knew this because the motto was on the sign at the highway exit for the town. Nicely calibrated, Cook, I thought. I drove the short way to the address Bentley had given me for the campaign headquarters. It was, unsurprisingly, in a half-empty strip mall. These formerly solid communities were plagued by the strip malls that had been built in their more affluent period and were now nearly abandoned.

I picked up my shoulder bag and walked up to the front door where "Steve Works for US!" posters were plastered and pushed on it.

Locked. Interesting.

A thin, thirtyish African American guy with horn-rimmed spectacles came hurrying toward the door with a key. He unlocked the door with a sheepish grin and held it wide for me.

"Ms. Ginelli?" he asked as I walked past him.

"Yes, and you must be Mr. Bentley," I said, keeping my voice soft and sweet.

"Right, right you are, ma'am. But you must call me Chris."

I shook his outstretched hand. He had quite a grip. Up closer, what I had taken for his thin frame was actually wiry muscle. He was tall for a gymnast. Perhaps a martial artist, I speculated silently. Or, I thought, a swimmer.

"Come right this way," he said, pointing down a narrow and not well-lit hall. "The candidate is in his office, and we're expecting you."

There was no receptionist at the front desk, I noted as we walked past.

Chris opened a door midway down the hall and announced, "Ms. Ginelli to see you sir."

A tall, white man with brown hair and distinguished strands of grey at his temples stood up. The grey strands were so perfect, I wondered if they were painted on. ·

As I shook his smooth, manicured hand, I had to remind myself to tamp down my hostility to this man who had allowed Alice and likely many other girls to be abused by Coach Larsen as he and others let the abusive coach move from team to team when there were complaints.

I took the proffered seat, a folding chair, and noted the Walmart office furniture. The candidate's desk was a cheap, plywood affair painted to look like wood, the padding on his office chair was worn, and the filing cabinets, of which there were many, were plastic.

"We're just getting moved in here," Cook said, noting my assessment of his office.

"Well, it is reassuring that you are not wasting money on frills when hopefully you will be moving to DC soon," I trilled.

"Right, right," Chris said. "How about some coffee?"

I was going to refuse. I could only imagine the coffee pot that matched this décor, and then I saw there was one of those take-out cartons from Starbucks on top of one of the filing cabinets.

"Certainly," I said. "I take it black."

Inside I chided myself. Suburban Ginelli would take cream in her coffee. Oh well.

When we all had coffee, Cook started into a standard spiel about his commitment to these communities, his desire to bring jobs to this region that had tragically lost so many over the years, the failures of his predecessors to do so and his own roots in the area.

It was so boring I was glad I had regular coffee and not decaf. I needed the caffeine to stay awake.

I finally couldn't stand it anymore and interrupted the flow.

"I saw on your website that you had been on the USA Swimming local association council that oversees the swim teams in this area. Did you find there were any problems like the issues they had in California?" I managed a blush by holding my breath a little, something one can do with Scandinavian skin. "I mean, you know, the girls and all being abused by coaches and the association councils just ignoring that?"

Chris was sitting just to my right, and I saw him stiffen. The candidate looked nonplussed for a minute, then he rallied.

"Oh no. No, no, no. Nothing like that. This isn't California, you know," he said, the sides of his mouth turning up in a parody of a smile.

"You know," I went on in what I hoped was a gossipy tone, "we've had a scandal at the university near where my husband and I live now. The swim coach there was found drowned, and the police decided it was murder. Larsen, I think his name was. You would have known him, right? He coached in your association for years."

"Well now," Cook harumphed. "At my level, on the council and all, it was not exactly like we were going to the swim meets. We had a much more executive role."

"Right," Chris contributed, I thought through clenched teeth.

"So, you didn't know him?" I asked leaning forward, dropping my own suburban mom act.

"Can't say that I did," Cook responded gruffly, standing up. The elderly desk chair squealed in protest.

"And you have that meeting downtown," Chris contributed, also standing.

"Well, thank you for your time and the coffee. I have two daughters and I am naturally concerned they stay safe," I said.

But I realized I wasn't fooling them. They were both glaring at me.

I headed out to the nearly empty parking lot and turned the car toward the side road that led to the entrance to the highway. It was after 2 and the roads would be worse than ever.

Going north it wasn't as bad as I feared, however, and soon I was rolling along at nearly 50, an unheard-of speed for that highway. I had time to consider both Cook's and Bentley's responses. First, Bentley wasn't so new to Cook that Larsen's misdeeds and the cover-ups were unknown to him. And Cook clearly knew about Larsen's death. That must be a relief to him, I thought. The window for reporting past abuse was open in Illinois, but it would not do much good to report someone who was dead. They could not defend themselves. Still, the rumor mill could . . .

Suddenly I felt a jolt from behind. A car with a tinted windshield had tapped my bumper. I put on my signal to pull to the side so we could exchange information, and the car that had bumped me swerved to my left and hit me from the side. I veered onto the shoulder and slowed abruptly, trying to get behind the car that was clearly aiming to run me off the road.

I sprayed up a lot of gravel and skidded some, but I kept control of my car. But by the time I had straightened out, the car that had hit me had sped up and dodged three lanes over toward an exit. I'd never catch it now.

I was shaken, and I took the next exit. I pulled into the parking lot of a Burger King and parked. I got out and assessed the damage. Subarus are sturdy cars, but I had sustained some serious body damage. The bumper was dented and scraped, and there was a long gash on the left rear door. I was glad I'd swerved away when I did or the other car could have bashed into the driver's side door, trapping, perhaps even injuring me.

I got my purse and went into the restaurant. I ordered a soft serve, vanilla cone and sat in a corner and licked it until my heartrate came down.

Had I encountered just another Dan Ryan crazy driver, or had it been deliberate, given my probing questions for the candidate? I didn't know, but I really felt it was related.

Before I went back to my car, I dialed Alice.

"Can you meet for coffee at 3:30?" I asked. "I've just been to that campaign office."

"Yeah," she said. "And Mel's patrolling today. I'll see if he can come by as well. Usual place?"

"Yes," I said. And I drove very carefully home.

* * *

The three of us huddled around an outdoor table at the coffee shop Alice liked.

Alice and I had drinks, mine decaf coffee, Alice's tea. Mel had declined a drink. He also thought meeting outside was, in his words, "nuts."

I quickly described what I had learned and then the suspicious attempt to run me off the road on my return.

"Still, could be the stupid Ryan," Mel said slowly.

"I know," I said. "But I made them very nervous. That is certain."

Alice was stone-faced.

"So, what?" I finally said. "You gonna say something?"

"There's no point. You gonna do what you gonna do. Whatever I say doesn't get through to you, you so stubborn."

I exploded.

"I'm stubborn? I'm stubborn? You look up stubborn in the dictionary, and it says Alice Matthews."

I saw Mel was smiling.

Alice and I both turned on him.

"It's like old times," he said. He got up and hustled off.

"I suppose it is," I said slowly.

"You know, Alice," I went on, "that campaign manager looked more than a little upset that I brought up Larsen. It's not only Cook we have to consider if eliminating Larsen was the plan."

"So, we need to find out where this Chris Bentley is from, and what's he doin' on a campaign for a white guy in that area. Doesn't make sense," Alice said thoughtfully and took out her little notebook.

I was so glad to see the little notebook I could have clapped my hands.

But I didn't. And she'd said "we."

27

~

It is not a lack of love, but a lack of friendship
that makes unhappy marriages.

— **Friedrich Nietzsche**

Tom and I talked well into the night about whether the attempt to run me off the road was random road rage or related to my questions for the candidate and his aide. Tom was very angry that I had been, yet again, in danger.

The girls' last feeding did not go well as I was upset. I had to ask Tom to leave our bedroom so I could relax. But after I finished and returned them to the nursery, we resumed the so-called "discussion." I just kept reiterating that he knew who I was before we married. I reminded him of when he had helped me get ready for stakeouts. He kept reiterating that was "before we had the girls."

That was the crux of it. The vulnerability of the babies was scary to him. It scared me too. But I felt if I gave in to his demand to "not put yourself in these dangerous positions" I would lose something fundamental about myself.

All I could come up with finally is "You need to trust me." He didn't reply, and we got ready for bed.

He was up and gone before I woke the next morning.

* * *

After everyone had left, I went to my study room intending to call the FBI agent I knew, Kamal Nadar, who dealt with cyberterrorism. As I sat down, my phone rang. "Number blocked" displayed on the phone. That was how the FBI called.

Speaking of scary, how did they know my schedule? Don't be paranoid, I told myself. Just a coincidence.

"Dr. Ginelli," Nadar's deep voice intoned over the cell phone.

"Hello, Agent Nadar. I was just going to call you about what is going on at my university."

"Yes. And that is why I am calling. I'd like to pay a visit to your campus today, see the office layout and talk with you, Dr. Turner, and Dr. Winters."

"I think I can arrange that, but it will have to be over the lunch break. Dr. Turner is spending this week teaching her intensive class, and it runs all morning and afternoon. There is, however, a 2-hour lunch break."

"So, Dr. Turner did not cancel her class after the threat?" he asked. I thought he was going for a nonjudgmental tone but didn't quite succeed.

"No," I said firmly. "That is not Dr. Turner's style."

"Well, call me back at a number I will text you, and let me know if that will be possible."

"Certainly. I need to get right on that as her class will be starting soon."

I hung up and immediately dialed Nia's cell phone. She answered on the first ring.

"Hi, Nia. I'll make this quick. An FBI agent I know, and trust to a certain degree, just called. He'd like to meet with you, Adelaide, and me over the noon hour and go over the investigation."

"You have interesting friends, Kristin," she said dryly.

I didn't want to go into how Agent Nadar had helped capture my husband's murderer.

"He's more of a longer-term acquaintance," I said slowly, "but I've had reason to trust his word."

"Alright, then. Keep in mind I'm not expecting too much."

"Yes, Nia, I can see why. I'll call Adelaide too and see if we can meet in the seminar room at noon."

"Good," she said. "Got to go," and she hung up.

I called Adelaide's cell, but it went to voicemail. I left a message for her to call me immediately though "not a crisis" was how I phrased it. I didn't want to jolt her too much.

I went upstairs and pulled out some fitted pants, blouse, and jacket that I hadn't had on in many months. The swimming was helping me slim down, and I was able to get into the pants, though just barely. I didn't put on the blouse, however, as I wanted to feed the girls one more time before I left for the office, and that could be a messy job. In fact, I thought, I'll leave the pants on the bed too, and I undressed and laid out my go to work clothes. I pulled on a nursing blouse and sweats for the rest of the morning.

My cell was on the bed too, and it rang as I was pulling on some house slippers.

"Kristin, what's up?" Adelaide said, her anxiety just below the surface.

I explained what Agent Nadar wanted and indicated Nia could join. Noon in the seminar room, I explained.

"Okay. Should I order sandwiches?" she said.

I pondered that. What tone did we want for this meeting? More relaxed couldn't hurt, I thought, though I'd never actually seen Agent Nadar relaxed. His tall frame with broad shoulders and slim waist was always ramrod straight. But a sandwich wouldn't hurt him.

"Yes, I think that's a good idea. I can order if you like."

"No, let me do it and charge it directly to the department account."

"Okay. I'll be over at about 11," I said, and we hung up.

I texted Nia the meeting was set, and there would be sandwiches.

"What kind of sandwiches go with FBI investigations?" she texted back.

I chuckled.

"Well, not turkey," I replied, and she sent a smile emoji.

* * *

I did manage to get to campus only a little after 11. Sandra was not in our shared office. She was taking the rest of January term to do a travel course to Antarctica with several students. I looked at her neatened up desk and wondered how they were faring. They were on a small ship, I knew, with several environmental experts aboard including Sandra to educate the tourists. The ship belonged to National Geographic. I had looked the trip up when she'd told me about it, and I'd looked at pictures of the small craft navigating between glaciers, one of which had been calving, i.e., collapsing into the water. It appeared very scary.

See, Tom, my mind said. I'm not the only one who does scary things.

I left my door open so I could see Nadar when he arrived. I spent the time tossing circulars, book catalogues, and snail mail I'd collected from our boxes in the hall.

When I got near the bottom of the pile, there was a single sheet of paper with cutout letters pasted on it.

"Do you know you will die very soon?" it read.

Great.

I pulled out a clear file envelope from my bottom drawer and used a tissue to slip the paper into it.

Show and tell for Nadar.

As I sat there contemplating the words through the plastic, I wondered if anyone else had gotten one of these. And I wondered why I had bothered to stop being a cop when clearly teaching at a university was nearly as dangerous.

Suddenly, the light coming in from the hall was blocked by a large shadow. I started a little. The moronic threat had put me on edge.

"Dr. Ginelli," Agent Nadar said. "May I come in?"

"Certainly," I said, and as he approached my desk, I silently handed him the plastic envelope.

He read it quickly.

"When did you get this?" he asked solemnly.

"I found it just now. I don't know how long it has been in my box or if anyone else has received one."

"I would like to call it in and get someone here to process your boxes and take this exhibit."

"Let's go down to the department chair's office and inform her," I said, rising.

I knocked on Adelaide's door, Agent Nadar right behind me. I was so jolted, I didn't even spare a glance for the coffee machine.

"Come in," Adelaide said. She was behind her desk, the light from the big, stained-glass window behind her spilling over on to her hair and shoulders making her look rather angelic. Nothing could be farther from the truth.

She rose and came toward us. I made the introductions, and she gestured us to sit.

"Not right this moment, ma'am," Agent Nadar said solemnly. "Dr. Ginelli found this in her mail," and he handed Adelaide the envelope. "I want to get someone here to process the other paper mail of your department. Indeed, I think we may need to sweep the whole building again."

"Oh my, yes," she said, the color draining from her face.

"I'll call now. Meanwhile, I think you all should vacate the building. Is there another building where you can go temporarily?"

"Maybe Hitchens," Adelaide said, picking up the phone. "It is the mirror building to this one on the other side of the quad. I don't think they are holding January term classes. Let me check."

She quickly dialed and determined from her department chair peer, this one in sociology, that their first-floor lounge and classroom were vacant.

"I will follow you there after we process this building," Agent Nadar said.

"I will get Nia and her class," I said quickly.

"I'll check to see if other faculty are in their offices," Adelaide said. And we set about the business of emptying our floor.

Nadar got off the phone.

"They're on their way. That team will take care of moving the others out and sweeping their floor."

"I'll relocate the sandwich delivery," Adelaide said.

I was amazed she could think of that at a time like this.

I hustled over to the seminar room and spoke quietly to Nia, asking her to come out into the hall. I explained I'd received a written threat and that the FBI would be sweeping the building. She could relocate her class to Hitchens, the building opposite, and their first-floor seminar room.

"Okay," she sighed and turned back into the room.

I hustled to get my bag and coat.

As I entered my office, I felt a mild buzzing in my ears and lightheadedness. I realized I had not had my usual shake when I was feeding the girls earlier. You're just dehydrated, I told myself, and grabbed a water bottle from the small fridge below my desk. Then I paused and grabbed a second one.

Guzzling water, I walked quickly down the stairs.

I felt a little better when I got to the quad, but I picked out a bench and sat down while I finished the water.

Babies, hormones, stress with Tom, Alice under investigation and these threats—was it too much for me? I prided myself on being strong and able to handle everything life threw at me. Was that helping or harming me now? And I hadn't handled Marco's murder, I realized. I'd quit the police force, gone to graduate school, and cared for my babies. Maybe I needed to retreat now.

Should I do that now? Retreat until I had my equilibrium back?

I can't. I can't, I thought. Alice. Nia. I have to have their backs.

I opened the second water and drank it while I trudged toward Hitchens.

* * *

As I entered Hitchens, I saw Adelaide and Nia in the seminar room. The students were not there.

Nia saw me through the door and gestured me in.

"I dismissed the students and told them I would put up an online lecture for this afternoon's work," she said, her face creased with concern.

"I think that's probably best," I said slowly and took a seat.

"I just hate to let these cowards get any kind of a win," she said through gritted teeth.

"Well, let's see what Agent Nadar has to say," Adelaide said, and she took a seat as well.

It took about an hour for Agent Nadar to join us. The sandwiches had been delivered but no one ate any. I took one of the soft drinks and drank it. The sugar helped.

Finally, Nadar put in an appearance.

"There were three other notes," he said without preamble. "You, Dr. Turner, Dr. Abubakar, and Dr. Winters. The notes have been sent to be processed, but unless there are clear fingerprints that are in our system, I do not expect very much. The security cameras had been requested after the bomb threat. I will do everything I can to expedite their installation.

"Do you have any questions?"

"Yes," Nia said, "I'd like your contact information so that my lawyer can speak with you."

"Certainly," he said and passed out cards.

"Another thing," I said. "Since the threats are escalating, I wonder if you will brief the president of the university and if you will recommend that the student whose blog posts kicked off this whole ruckus be expelled?"

"I have a meeting with the president this afternoon. I can certainly point out the connections, but once these threats start to escalate, one expulsion will not end them."

"I know that," Nia said, "but it sends a message nevertheless."

"I agree," I said.

"I as well," Adelaide contributed.

"I will certainly make that point," Nadar said solemnly. "Things normally go from bad to worse."

Oh. Great.

* * *

"Tom," I said as we were starting to get into bed. "I'd like to talk with you. I did some thinking today, and I don't yet feel like myself. What would really help me out is to feel you had my back when I am pursuing what I think is right. I need you in my corner."

"Kristin," Tom said slowly. "I see that, but I get so worried for you. It's hard for me to go back to the way we were and just wave at you when you go off with the FBI to make an arrest."

"I need that, though, Tom. I need that to continue to be myself. Can you try to back me up, and I will try to discuss things with you in advance?"

"Yes," he said, after a pause. "I think we need a new way."

As I snuggled in his arms, I felt better. Not completely better, but better. Progress.

28

Seventh and finally, the person has reconstructed a coherent system of meaning and belief that encompasses the story of trauma.

— **Judith Lewis Herman**, *Trauma and Recovery*

SH: Good to see you. How have these last weeks been?

AM: Better, I think, though it's weird.

SH: What's weird?

AM: Well, Kristin, you know her, got me this appointment."

SH: Yes.

AM: Right. Well, as is typical of her she's runnin' around tryin' to find who really did for that guy.

SH: Does it trouble you to say his name?
(Pause)
AM: Yeah, some.

SH: That's okay. Just another thing to work on at some point. So, Kristin is trying to find his murderer?

AM: Yeah. Exactly. And you'd think it'd make me feel worse, but it doesn't. And she's found all this stuff about how much coaches are getting away with, not just here but you know, in other places and how it's a pattern. You know, Dr. Hill, there's so much of it. So much. It makes me so angry, and I wanna do something about it.

SH: I know. It can seem like it's everywhere.

AM: Exactly! So now I'm doin' my own research and seein' how they operate, these guys. And I think I see why he was a threat to somebody. And how he got away with it for so long.

SH: You are taking over the investigation.

AM: Well, not taking over exactly, but doin' it. And pushin' forward. Kristin's still not 100% with her twins and all. And she gets pulled into other stuff. I need to push on this. And my partner, Mel, Mel Billman, he's totally in. I'm not alone in lookin' into all of it.

SH: Are there any trigger points for you, like what kinds of things can make you feel a little panic?

AM: Well, readin' about all that's happened with girls and women reporting. I feel like, I don't know, a pull toward the panic. It's out there, but it's not got me, if you get that. I can breathe and keep it away, out there like. You know?

SH: I think I do.

AM: I don't think we're done yet, though.

SH: Why is that?

AM: Because when we find his murderer, that will be what you call a trigger.

SH: I think you're right.

AM: So, I'll text you when we do and come see you.

SH: You sound confident you'll find his murderer.

AM: Oh yes. Me, Kristin, and Mel. Nobody gonna escape us for long. Nobody ever has.

29

~

Criticism may not be agreeable, but it is necessary. It fulfils the same function as pain in the human body. It calls attention to an unhealthy state of things.

—Winston Churchill

I HAD SLEPT BETTER after Tom's and my talk, but I was up early to feed the girls. Mrs. Brown gave them bottles during the night, but that meant my milk would come in heavily early in the morning.

Olivia was still not nursing as vigorously as Natalie, and I worried some about that. I was glad about the professional pediatric scale Tom had gotten, and after their feeding I'd asked him to weigh the girls this morning. Natalie still weighed more than Olivia, but that had been true from birth. The good news this morning was that Olivia was keeping pace and gaining appropriate ounces. We had both breathed a sigh of relief at that. Tom dutifully recorded the weight, height, time, and date.

What would I do without him? I thought as I watched him reassure each baby as he checked them.

Midmorning, I headed for the campus police station. Mel, Alice, and I had arranged to meet.

They were both there when I arrived, sitting at the small table by the wall. Mel had some papers in front of him that it seemed he and Alice had been examining. He pushed them under a legal pad as I entered. What were they discussing he didn't want me to see? Then I chided myself for being like a tween girl, jealous of my friends' friendship. Still the hormones, I guessed.

"So, what's up?" I said, shrugging off my puffy, Chicago winter coat before I overheated and collapsed. I hung it up.

"Well," Mel said, his long fingers holding a pen and then starting to tap it on the legal pad, "we think the most promising lead is your getting nearly run off the road after you visited the candidate's office."

"Yeah," Alice added. "Like you usually do, you created some mess, but it works. Well, some of the time, anyway."

I thought for a minute.

"I think you're right, and I need to go back there, confront the candidate directly about those complaints that perhaps had been systematically ignored when he was on the council. I've got to question that campaign manager too, come to think of it. Dirt like covering up sexual abuse of teenage girls by his guy could really tank the campaign. The manager's got a stake in concealing that too," I said slowly picturing their furious faces when I'd last been there.

"I can head there tomorrow," I said, "but I don't think I'll make an appointment. I'll check his campaign schedule and hope I'll catch them in the office and off guard. My last lecture for Nia is not until the end of the week."

"Good," Mel said, making a note on his pad. "We can't neglect the swim team, though. From what you say, Kristin, that coach was harassing current team members. We need to dig further into that."

"Maybe not just team members," Alice said slowly, looking down at her nails. I noticed they were ragged from being bitten. Not like her. She usually kept her nails trimmed short and neat.

She saw me looking at her hands and put them under the table.

"What about that assistant coach you told us about, Kristin?" she said abruptly. "She could have heard something, seen something, hell he likely hit on her too, come to think of it."

I noticed Alice had started to breathe more deeply. Give her a minute, I thought. Anything about that swim team really seemed to upset her. Instead of replying, I got up and went to the credenza next to the far wall.

"Tea or coffee, anybody?" I asked, assessing what was available. There was a pot of coffee, but the machine looked like it had been brewing coffee since the university was founded. Tea was a safer bet. I checked the pot for water, and it was nearly full. I turned it on.

I came back to the table. Mel saw what I had done and gave me a quick nod. Alice was still concentrating on her breathing.

She shook herself. Then she narrowed her eyes at me.

"So, you get anything when you were at the pool from that assistant?"

"Not really, no," I said, starting to feel a little defensive. "I hardly spoke to her."

"Why not?" Alice persisted.

"Well, I just didn't," I said, even more defensive.

"Dropped the ball on that, Kristin. I'll follow up," Alice said briskly.

Whoa. Alice had criticized me before, but not like this, not with all this judgment. Now I was the one who needed to take a breath.

"Good," I said curtly.

Mel looked from one to the other of us and pointedly tapped his pad.

"So, I'll try to talk to students who use the exercise facility up the street," he said firmly. "It's open 24 hours, and they're there at all hours, perhaps they saw a car the night that guy drowned. Or even better, maybe some were taking selfies for God knows what reason and caught that part of the street."

"Good," Alice said firmly. She turned to me.

"Kristin, what's the name of that assistant coach again?"

"Amanda Parkinson," I said shortly.

Alice gave me one of her looks, the kind that said, "I know you're pissed but too damn bad."

Once again, I felt like teenage girl, prickly and stupid. Not right. Alice was stepping up, and I needed to acknowledge that. I really had dropped the ball on Parkinson. As I thought about it, I'd been influenced by Ms. Sanchez's view, and I should have done my own investigation.

"She's easy to recognize," I added. "Stick thin with a tuft of orange hair on the top of her head."

"Good. Thanks. That helps," Alice said, now giving me a half smile.

"Okay, then," Mel said standing up and pulling his coat from the back of his chair. "It's a plan. We'll meet back here at the end of the week and compare notes."

I thought he couldn't get out of the room fast enough.

After he left, I looked at Alice. Then I heard the tea kettle.

"Tea?" I asked.

"Yeah," she replied. She looked a lot more tired than when I'd first gotten to the office.

* * *

I walked home, nursed the babies, read to them again in their bounce chairs and then fixed myself a sandwich after they'd fallen asleep. I sat in our new family room watching them sleep. I need to take more time to enjoy them now, I thought. They are this little for such a short time.

I took the girls back to the nursery and managed to get them down without waking them. I took a moment to fill Mrs. Brown in on the successful weigh-in this morning, and I could tell she was very pleased. As I left the room, she sat down in the rocker there and picked up a novel she had been reading. J.D. Robb. We had that in common.

The walk back to campus could have been worse. For January in Chicago, that's the best you can say. A west wind blew across the flat expanses of open spaces and then, just when you got a moment of relief from a building blocking the gale, it blasted back out at you from alleys between the structures. At least there was no sleet or snow. Like I thought, best you can do.

I struggled to open the heavy door of Myerson. The wind wanted to keep it shut. Finally, a student coming out pushed it toward me, and I got in. I still hadn't regained my pre-baby strength, I realized, despite the swimming.

As I reached our floor, I saw Agent Nadar knocking on Nia's office door. I heard her say "Who is it?" and Nadar replied with his name. The sound of a lock disengaging reassured me that Nia was still security conscious.

"Good afternoon, Professor," Agent Nadar said as she was framed in the door.

"Hello, Kamal," Nia said in a very welcoming voice. "I'm so glad you could make it."

Now that's really interesting, I said to myself as I scanned my new keycard at my office.

30

~

It's turtles all the way down.

—attributed to Bertrand Russell

Mel

The frigid air stole his breath. Why do these students go exercise at midnight, he wondered. Because they can, he answered himself. They want to feel their freedom.

As he hurried across the campus toward the exercise facility, he glanced up. The moon's edges were made sharp by the glacial cold. This moon was what his Diné wife called a Waxing Crescent. Well, she called it that in English. He'd never quite got the hang of her first language, Navajo, but he loved to hear her say the words as she sprinkled pollen in the morning.

He chuckled to himself. Better not let Mama hear me say that.

As he came out of the shelter of the quadrangle buildings and started to walk across the frozen lawn, he could see the three levels of the exercise facility lit up brightly. The tall windows on each level framed the people running, lifting weights, standing around conversing.

He reached the entrance but did not go in. Instead, he took out his phone, freed a finger from his glove, and took a picture toward the aquatics center, dark now, as it was not open after 11 pm. There was empty street parking that far down the street, as he'd thought there would be. He took several pictures in that direction. Then he turned and started asking people coming out the door of the athletic facility. If this were their regular schedule, they might have been here on the night of the murder.

"Did you exercise the night of . . . .? Did you see anyone down by the aquatics center? Were there any cars parked down there this late?" He mostly picked out students to ask because they might, just might, have decided to take some selfie with a friend when they exited with the dark pool building behind them.

After 45 minutes of freezing my ass off, I've got nothing, he thought. He went inside the building to warm up. He continued to ask the trickle of people heading for the exit.

Finally, one guy, looked African American and likely a grad student, said, "Maybe."

Mel tried not to show too much interest.

"What did you see?"

"Well, that building is closed at about 11, I think, and I remember thinking it was odd that there was a car parked down there."

"What kind of car, do you recall?"

"Well, I'm kind of a car guy, so yeah. It was a ten-year-old Honda. Probably dark blue but looked black at night. I noted it because those older Hondas have trouble with oil dilution problems with gas getting into the oil when it's freezing outside, and it was bitter that night. I wondered if the car wouldn't start when the person got back to it. Just a passing thought, really." He started walking away. Then he paused and said over his shoulder, "That age, a Toyota is a better bet."

"Thanks," Mel said with a chuckle to himself. Just needed to find a car enthusiast.

* * *

Kristin

The next morning, I had just finished nursing the girls when my text tone sounded.

"So that's what I got. 10-year-old dark blue Honda. Maybe. Mel."

Well, it was something. Mel had texted me and Alice together, so I hit reply and let them both know I was headed to the southside congressional candidate's office. His website had not shown he had any events today, though of course he and his campaign manager both could have meetings that would not be listed publicly that would take them out of the office.

As I drove, I contemplated a little breaking and entering if they were not there, though I was on the fence about that. I'd done it before, and Anna had lectured me severely after freeing me from police custody.

I need to dial it back, I thought.

In the mid-morning, the traffic was not hideous and soon I was tooling down the side road toward the nearly abandoned strip mall and the candidate's office.

There was a car already parked in front. I was not a car expert like the guy Mel had found at the exercise facility, but it looked like an older model to me. It was dark blue and as I walked around the front of it, the H for Honda was on the front. Well, well.

I got out my phone and took a photo of the car from the back, being sure to get the license plate.

The door to the offices was shut. No one was at the reception desk again. I knocked and waited. No reply. I pushed on the door, and it opened. Not locked.

No wonder no one heard me, I realized, as there was the buzzcut sound of a shredder going full blast.

Could be harmless shredding of old materials or it could be someone getting rid of compromising files.

I tiptoed down the hall toward where the sound was coming from and peeked in. It was another office with a peeling, laminated desk and two folding chairs. There was a stack of partly broken-down legal boxes next to a medium-sized shredder that was going full blast.

Then I heard footsteps, and I hurried in and crouched behind the desk.

The campaign manager came in with a substantial stack of the same kind of old boxes on a dolly. He dumped them on the floor next to the others and hurried out, trailing the dolly behind him.

When he'd gone, I came out from behind the desk and peeked in the top box. "Confidential Report" was written on the top of a cover sheet. I picked it up and flipped through the pages. It was clearly a complaint about the behavior of Harold Larsen as coach of the Midlothian swim team.

Bingo.

I stacked up as many boxes as I thought I could carry and hurried out to my car. I popped the trunk and shoved them in. Then I came back and when I'd opened the front door, I listened. I could hear thumps from further down the hall. More boxes were being dragged out to be put on the dolly.

I ducked into the shredder room and grabbed another stack.

I'll probably get a hernia from this, I thought, as I hefted the huge pile of boxes into my arms. I staggered out to my car and unceremoniously dumped the new stack into the trunk. I slammed it shut.

Then I jumped behind the wheel and took off, back down the side road.

When I reached the entrance to the highway, I pulled off into a McDonald's parking lot. I parked in the far corner and popped the trunk again. I needed to look in all the boxes to make sure I wasn't absconding with the candidate's previous years' tax returns.

I took each box out and placed it on dry areas of the macadam of the adjacent parking place. I opened each one and dug down all the way to the bottom, pulling out documents at random. Each box had the same cover sheets but the dates on them varied by year. It was appalling. Complaint after complaint, all stored and likely never acted upon.

I loaded all the boxes back into my trunk and slammed it shut. As I started for the highway, I thought of the story often attributed to Bertrand Russell of a scientist who gives a lecture about the Earth's position in the universe. An elderly woman in the audience argues that the Earth is actually supported on the back of a giant turtle. When asked what the turtle is standing on, she replies that it's another turtle. When pressed further, she insists that it's "turtles all the way down."

I used the story in my introductory religion classes to illustrate the concept of infinite regress, the idea that every explanation needs a further explanation.

The abuse of women and girls throughout history was turtles all the way down. Or rather, it was lies and corruption all the way down.

31

After a traumatic experience, the human system of self-preservation seems to go onto permanent alert, as if the danger might return at any moment.

— **Judith Lewis Herman**, *Trauma and Recovery*

I TEXTED MEL AND Alice, and they came over in the afternoon to help me carry the boxes from the trunk of my car into my house. I thought putting them in the basement was best. It was quite dry, as I'd had the walls and floor painted with a waterproof sealant when I first moved in. I stored several folding tables down there for backyard picnics, so we were able to open those up and stack the boxes on them.

There were nine boxes in all.

When we'd gotten them all on to the tables, we stood around looking at these dented, lopsided cardboard containers like they were ticking.

Alice's grim face was blotchy in places, I thought from stress, though the overhead, exposed bulb lighting was likely making us all look like zombies.

"Let's get some tea or coffee upstairs and make a plan," I said in a faux cheery voice.

"Yeah," Mel said. He saw how hard this was on Alice.

"I only have an hour," she rasped out. "We need to get on with it."

I sighed.

"Fine," I said, "but we need to make a plan, nevertheless. Shall we see what's in each box and sort them by date?"

"Okay," Mel agreed walking up to the table closest to him and taking the cover off of a box.

"Oh, wait," I said. "We'll need paper and pencil to make a list of the contents and a marker to label each box on the top and side once we've looked at it. Let me go get that."

I ran up the stairs to my study room and grabbed what we needed. On the way back through the kitchen, I picked up three bottles of water and hurried back down.

I gave out the waters and placed some of the markers, pads, and pens on each table.

It was quiet as we each started to go through a box.

"2008 to 2009," Mel said in a monotone, and he selected a marker and wrote on that box.

"2011 to 2013," I said getting to the bottom of the box I was working on. Then I looked up. Alice looked like she was going to get into that freezing thing she did. She was breathing hard, and there were little, intermittent gasps between the deep breaths.

I just went over to the side wall, grabbed a folding chair, opened it, and put it behind her legs. She folded into it. I opened one of the waters.

"Just drink it, okay?"

She did, but with a jerky movement of her arm and hand like she was having to tell her muscles what to do.

"2007," she said in a low voice. "The year I was on that team. Saw name. I knew her. I never knew she'd been, you know, whatever." She bowed her head and whispered. "There's just so many of them. So many."

"Drink some more water," I said in a neutral tone, "and then we can write that down on the pad and label the box."

Her shoulders dropped some. A little tension was leaving her body.

"Yeah. Right. That's the thing to do."

I looked over at Mel, and he had his own frozen face on. Then he just picked up one of the pads and a pen and took it over to Alice. He put it on the table in front of her where there was a space between boxes and returned to where he had opened another carton.

"Thanks," Alice said quietly.

We worked in silence for nearly an hour until we had lists of what was in each box and the dates. So many small, southside towns. So many coaches. So many of the same names of young women year after year. So much pain disregarded, boxed, and buried. I felt a kind of burning rage, the kind I felt when I saw the body of an innocent person murdered by some creep.

I looked over at Alice. She had gotten up from the chair and done two boxes, listing names, dates, and locations on the pad, then labeling the box. Her body was terrible to look at, rigid with tension, and her eyes sunken in her increasingly thin face.

"Okay, then, that's it, right?" I said after the top had been put on the last box. "Let's go upstairs."

I collected the three pads, the pens and the markers and followed Alice and Mel up the stairs. Before I shut off the light, I turned and looked at the tables with the boxes. The picnic tables were white, and it could have been a morgue containing small bodies. Perhaps in a way it was.

I put out some bread, condiments, and cold cuts on the center island. Mel joined me in making a sandwich, but Alice just sat down at the table with her empty bottle of water. I put the tea kettle on hoping I could get her to drink some tea with sugar.

I fixed Alice's tea, set it in front of her, and Mel and I carried our food over.

Alice took a sip of her tea.

"You tryin' to rot my teeth?" she said, putting the tea back down.

"Yes, Alice. That was my goal," I said smiling.

"It's working," she said after she sipped again.

We sat in silence for a while.

"Can we use this stuff?" Mel finally asked.

"I don't know," I said slowly. "Since I effectively stole it, can it be used under that new law in Illinois that re-opens the window for reporting? I'll have to ask my lawyer friend."

"Could be used if we contact all those women, ask 'em, and they say yes," Alice said.

Mel and I looked at her. It wasn't every day you saw courage in the raw.

* * *

I fed the girls after Mel and Alice left and then took a quick shower and changed. The boxes had been dirty in more ways than one.

After that, I headed for my office. I wanted to check in with Nia and see if she'd heard anything from Agent Nadar about the search for the person who'd left the threatening notes, perhaps the same person who'd made the bomb threats.

I hurried up the stairs of Myerson and heard voices coming from Nia's office. One was very deep, likely the sonorous voice of Agent Nadar. I knocked.

"Who is it?" Nia asked through the door.

"It's me, Kristin. I wanted to check in with you."

She opened the door, and Agent Nadar was rising from the seating arrangement in the corner of the office.

"Hello, Dr. Ginelli," Nadar said.

"Hello, Agent Nadar," I said, and I couldn't conceal a small smile. There were two take-out sandwich boxes and two half-empty cups of coffee on the coffee table near where they'd clearly been sitting.

"Come join us," Nia said, clearly noting that I had taken in the impromptu luncheon arrangement. She always looked well pulled together in a professional way, but I thought the earrings and necklace she was wearing became her very well, framing her elegant face and neck.

"I don't want to disturb you, but I wondered if there had been any news on our would-be bomber and perhaps also the person who put out those notes."

"Yes, I have an update," Nadar said, resuming his seat. "I just dropped by to let Nia know that when we searched the library where that student blogger has his own locked carrel, we found a burner phone hidden in the heating register under the fixed desk. It was the phone used to make the bomb threat. Also, our handwriting experts have told us that samples of his handwriting match the notes left in the faculty boxes here. His attempt to disguise that was very poorly done. I have, of course, let your department chairperson know this already."

I looked over at Nia. She nodded.

"So, what will happen to him?" I asked.

"He has been arrested, and it is my understanding he will be expelled from the university. His so-called blog has been taken into evidence and is no longer functioning."

Well, that was good news, I thought as I thanked Kamal and told Nia we'd talk later. I left them to finish their lunch, and I went back to my office and sat down to think.

The next thing that needed to be done was to get rid of that ghastly "free speech" policy.

I turned on my computer and emailed Adelaide asking if we could meet to strategize how to negotiate a review of that policy through the proper university channels.

Then I turned my attention to reviewing my other emails, the flotsam and jetsam of university life flowing into my inbox like so much wastewater. It had to be emptied though.

A new email popped up from Adelaide at the top of the page.

"University channels be damned. I have called and requested a meeting with the university president. We need to just put pressure on him to suspend and ultimately cancel that policy. You good with that?"

"Yes. Count me in," I emailed back.

32

Unlike simple stress, trauma changes your view of your life and yourself. It shatters your most basic assumptions about yourself and your world — "Life is good," "I'm safe," "People are kind," "I can trust others," "The future is likely to be good" — and replaces them with feelings like "The world is dangerous," "I can't win," "I can't trust other people," or "There's no hope."

— Mark Goulston MD

Alice, that evening

Alice parked across the street from the aquatics facility. She watched the young women on the team exit in twos and threes. Their youthful voices traveled in the freezing air, excited, happy, pumped. "Okay now, that was dope." "Yeah, gonna crush State." "Did you see Janet make that turn at the end? Looked like a dolphin!"

They seem a million miles away from me, Alice thought.

She worked on her breathing. Don't wanna freeze. I can do this, she thought. In, out. Control. She reached into her pocket and brought out a small container of Vicks VapoRub she had used for Shawna when she'd gotten that bronchitis. She'd read some about this PTSD, the triggers. Smell was a big one for her. The smell of chlorine got her right back there with him. She tucked a dab in each nostril and sniffed. Good. Smelled awful but not like a pool.

She crossed the street toward the lighted foyer. She hadn't seen the assistant coach, Amanda Parkinson, leave yet. She hadn't wanted to make an appointment with Parkinson and give her time to worry, or to duck the meeting, she thought wryly.

She walked through the foyer and waited for the smell of the pool to hit her. All she smelled was that strong menthol that filled all her sinus area. It was working. The Internet's not always wrong, she thought.

Her boots squeaked on the streaks of water that were closer to the pool.

"Somebody there?" a high-pitched voice called from an office down a short, side corridor.

"Hello," Alice called in what she hoped was a reassuring voice. "It's Officer Matthews from the campus police. Can I talk to you for a minute?"

A young woman appeared in the doorway of an office. She was so thin she looked like one of those sparkle sticks the kids liked on July 4, complete with a flame on top because her hair was so bright orange.

"I spoke to the police. I don't have anything more to say," she said jerkily, starting to close the door.

"I just have a few follow-ups," Alice said gently, putting a foot in the doorway but not blocking the door. "May I come in and sit with you for a few minutes? It is mightily cold outside."

"Well. I guess," she said, her voice still high from tension, but she stepped aside so Alice could enter. She sat down on a desk chair and gestured to a ragged loveseat across the small room.

Oh, loveseat, Alice thought. Not a good furnishing in here. I can't sit there. She grabbed a straight back chair by the wall and put it in front of the loveseat. Memories could flood in if she sat on that little couch. She took off her winter uniform coat and as she hung it on the back of the chair, she turned her phone to record.

She sat down and looked over at the young woman whose body language was nearly armored. Amanda had crossed her legs, twisting them to one side, and she'd crossed her arms over her chest while hunching her back and tucking her chin. Alice's heart went out to her. No amount of self-protection would keep the predators at bay though.

"So, I've got work," she said. "What're your questions?"

Alice took a deep breath.

"Amanda, I was on a swim team in a southern suburb. Larsen was our coach. He hurt me, and I think he hurt many others. I think he may have hurt you or you saw him hurt some of the girls. Am I right?"

Amanda's body jerked up like she had received an electric shock. She was on her feet in seconds, clearly poised to flee. Alice recognized the flight response. She tried to channel her therapist's calm.

"It won't work, you know," she said slowly in a low voice to the trembling woman. "You can't run from those memories. They go with you. I know. I know all too well."

"No," Amanda said in a little girl's voice. "I don't wanna."

"I know. I know," Alice said. "You said no but he didn't listen."

"No, no. I don't wanna," Amanda said again. But she sat back down and hung her head.

"It was scary, wasn't it, never knowing when he'd come at you?"

"Yes."

Alice let the silence continue for a little bit.

"I started leaving with the girls on the team and then coming back in the evening after I thought he'd left. Get the rest of my work done," Amanda said hollowly.

"That was smart," Alice said gently.

"Yeah, maybe. But that night . . . ." She trailed off.

"The night he died?" Alice asked quietly.

"Yeah. Yeah. I heard yelling coming from the weight room. You know it? It's down the hall on the other side of the pool. I recognized his voice and some other guy. Coach was yelling, yelling so loud I heard him like he was next to me. 'You pay up or I'll spill it all. I'll tell what I did and be damned. I got this cancer, and I ain't gonna live that long anyway. I can leave something to my kids. You pay me or your boy is toast. And I know he kept those complaints. I went to see him first and demanded money. He showed me a closet with boxes. He said, 'There's my cross. I drag it around with me.' So, your boy is wacko, though I guess you know that already."

That must be the boxes Kristin found, Alice thought.

"Like a penance, you know?" Amanda said. "I was raised Catholic, and I know all about that. That candidate guy kept the complaints he'd never done anything about like a penance." She shuddered.

Alice waited while Amanda hugged herself again.

"So, I left my office and hid in the closet where we keep the swim fins, floats, kickboards, and all. I have a key. It's right behind the bench along the side of the pool, the side by this office corridor.

"Finally, it got really quiet. I waited in the closet for a while and then I opened the door and peeked out."

She started to breathe really fast. Alice was afraid she would hyperventilate. She saw the edge of a crumpled brown bag in the trashcan by the desk and went and got it. The remnants of what must have been Amanda's lunch were still in it. She dumped that out and held the bag so the young woman could breathe into it.

"Breathe into this. Slow and easy. Come on now. You can do it."

Slowly Amanda's breathing returned to normal.

"So, so I saw this guy," she continued. "He was like tall, maybe thirty, sort of medium brown skin, and he was dragging Coach Larsen by the feet. The coach's head was wrapped in a towel. The man dragged him right up to the pool, put his feet in the water, pulled off the towel and slid him right down into the water. As the man stood up, I shut the door. If he'd seen me, oh God, if he'd seen me . . ."

Her whole body shook.

"It's okay. It's okay. Clearly, he didn't see you. You're safe, you're doing fine. It's okay," Alice said.

"So after about half an hour, I cracked the door. The lights were still on in the pool area. I listened and didn't hear anyone. I came out and looked in the pool. Coach was face down in the water. I knew he was dead."

She almost choaked on a sob.

"I was glad."

Alice put her hand on the back of the young woman's hand. It was ice cold.

"Amanda, I think I need to take you to the Emergency Room. You've had a bad shock hearing and seeing all that and now remembering it."

"No, no. No doctors. I can't tell. I mustn't tell."

"You don't have to tell them anything. Believe me, I know. They will help you," Alice said.

"I feel so dizzy." Amanda started to slide sideways out of the chair.

Alice grabbed her shoulders and levered her slowly to the floor. She put the young woman's feet up on the chair.

Blankets, Alice thought. I need blankets. Or maybe towels. She told Amanda she'd be right back, and she ran toward the shower area. She opened a big closet right before the turn into the shower area, and there were piles of towels. She grabbed as many as she could carry and hurried back.

She spread the towels all over Amanda and even wrapped her head to get her warm. She chafed her hands and then tucked them in as well.

After about 15 minutes, Alice thought, I should call the EMT's.

Then Amanda stirred and struggled to sit up.

"Easy now, easy," Alice said, and she helped her sit back, leaning on the wretched loveseat.

While Amanda had been warming up, Alice had searched the little office and found a kettle in a drawer along with some mugs, tea, instant coffee, and sugar. She went out to a drinking fountain down the hall and got water. Soon she had a cup of hot tea with a ton of sugar in it ready for Amanda.

Just like that sugar tea Kristin made for me, she thought wryly.

Alice handed her the mug, and Amanda obediently sipped the tea.

"Listen, Amanda," Alice said. You know you've had a shock. If you won't go to the Emergency Room, I'll drive you home. You need to rest then. But seriously, you need to talk to someone about what happened to you. I've written a name and number on this piece of paper. Call her."

Amanda took the paper with a shaking hand.

"My bike, it's here."

"It'll keep," Alice said, and she pulled Amanda's coat from the office closet.

As Alice supported Amanda out to her car, the young woman whispered to her, "You know that woman, the blond who swims? She saw there was a weight missing from the weight room. I saw it too, the next day. I checked. Do you think that's how he did it?"

Alice could feel the shudders wracking her thin frame.

"Don't think about that now. Plenty of time for that later," Alice said sternly.

* * *

Early the next morning in Kristin's basement

Alice had called me at dawn and said she had important evidence to share. She'd also called Mel, and they wanted to come over and meet in the basement. So, at 6 am I held the two girls and started to nurse them while Alice played us the tape.

"Please, stop the tape," I said as Natalie started to fuss. I was so upset after listening to what that poor young woman was saying, my milk had stopped letting down.

"Let me just take the babies upstairs to the nanny," I said. "Sorry."

"No, it's okay," Alice said. "It's horrible."

Mrs. Brown took my explanation of my milk slowing down matter-of-factly, and she just carried on, fixing two bottles.

When I got back to the basement, Alice and Mel were sitting by one of the picnic tables in silence.

"Okay, thanks," I said.

Alice switched the tape back on. It ran to the end. Penance, I thought. For God's sake, so to speak.

"So, we know who, and we know how," Mel said. "But how do we get this to the cops?"

"I say we play this for Gutierrez, get his advice," Alice said slowly.

"You can't do that Alice, making that recording was a crime," I said. "You'll need to transcribe it, show him and anyone else we consult your so-called 'notes,' and you can leave out that part about you," I said.

Mel nodded vigorously.

"Yeah, yeah. I'll write it up and then destroy the tape. I know this is a dual consent state. Not great, no, but I'll put in some about myself. I will. I'm gettin' better at that. It happened you know, and we all know it's relevant to the investigation. The shame is on that coach, not on me. That's a fact."

Mel and I looked at each other and then we nodded at Alice.

"I'll make the call," Mel said, and he went upstairs.

"Alice," I started.

"No, Kristin, don't. I know what you want to say but right now I need to be quiet for a bit."

"Sure," I said.

33

The legal system is designed to protect men from the superior power of the state but not to protect women or children from the superior power of men. It therefore provides strong guarantees for the rights of the accused but essentially no guarantees for the rights of the victim. If one set out by design to devise a system for provoking intrusive post-traumatic symptoms, one could not do better than a court of law.

— **Judith Lewis Herman**, *Trauma and Recovery*

Alice, Mel, and I had an appointment with Captain Gutierrez in two hours, but I was downtown at Anna's office. Alice was rightly concerned about how fragile Amanda Parkinson was and what would happen if she were questioned by the police. From what I had seen of Detective Booth, he might just turn his attention to another handy woman as his prime suspect if she admitted to being on the scene of the murder.

The question was how to protect this vulnerable woman while also getting Booth to act on her information.

I had given Anna a xeroxed copy of Alice's notes on what Amanda Parkinson had told her.

"That's a lot of detail," Anna commented when she'd finished reading.

"Alice immediately wrote it all down," I said. "And she has a very good memory."

Anna gave me the look that made lying witnesses cave on the stand, but I kept mum.

She cleared her throat.

"Well, anyway, that young woman could be shredded by an aggressive detective," she said. "You are right to be concerned." She tapped her pen on the legal pad in front of her, her manicured nails and intricate rings flashing in the overhead light.

"Amanda Parkinson can certainly have a lawyer with her, but as to a therapist. That's more of a grey area if they consider her a suspect."

Tap. Tap. Tap.

Anna always did that when she was thinking. It was kind of a mental metronome.

"So, the first task is to get her a pro bono lawyer. I have some ideas on that. Then the lawyer can interview her and make a case to the detectives that she is such a vulnerable witness she needs a therapist with her."

Anna started to rise.

"Ah, well, there's one more thing," I said, and I told her about "finding" the boxes of complaints at the campaign office. I'd taken them to keep them from being destroyed.

"Nonetheless, that is stealing if you took them off the premises without permission. And you still have them?" Anna said, turning to a new page on her pad.

"Yes, they're in my basement. Anna, there are so many, years and years of them. And that guy, the former swimming official, telling the Larsen guy he had kept them as penance. Really twisted."

"Well, I think Alice Matthews has the right idea of contacting the former complainants and seeing if they want to act now in this window that has opened in Illinois. That way the actual documents might not need to even come into it."

Tap. Tap. Tap.

"Indeed, it could become a huge case given how many you say there are. I can emphasize that with the lawyer I have in mind."

"Well, thanks. I do need to get to the meeting with the campus police captain. I can let him know at least about a lawyer for Parkinson. And then the lawyer will negotiate the therapist, right?"

"Yes, that's right," Anna said, rising.

"Kristin," she said as I was turning to leave, "I know you like to charge around trying to save people, but don't do anything like taking those boxes again, okay? Saving a person who is about to be killed is one thing, but saving documents is still not a good enough reason for a break in."

Anna was referring to another case where I had broken into a makeshift clinic to save a woman who was being kept in a coma so her organs could be trafficked.

"Well, to be fair, Anna, the door to the campaign office was open. I didn't break in."

"You know what I'm saying. Just don't do things like that, okay?" she said.

"Yes, I know," I said. Even to my own ears I sound petulant, I thought, like a teenager reprimanded for using her iPhone when she should have been studying.

Grow up, Kristin, I said to myself as I rode down in the elevator. You have five kids. You need to act like it.

* * *

Captain Gutierrez was reading the notes Alice had transcribed before she had erased the tape. Gutierrez had more grey in his mustache even than when I'd last seen him, but the large growth of hair above his lip was as expressive as ever. It went up and down and occasionally to one side or another as he perused the papers in front of him.

"Well, this certainly wraps it," he said. "Just about an eyewitness account."

He frowned at us but spoke directly to Alice.

"She as unsteady as she sounds, Officer Matthews? You know, if she's too flaked out, that Booth can just say you coerced her into it because she's another victim."

I heard Alice sharply draw in her breath. I was shocked too, though not surprised as I thought about it. High pressure police interrogation could just shred the little bit of control people with PTSD were able to manage.

"I'm getting her a lawyer to go with her, Captain, and we hope," I said, and I glanced at the colleagues, "I hope he or she will be able to get the detective to agree to have a therapist present."

The frown dragged the mustache nearly down to his chin.

"Long shot," he finally said. "Really long shot. They hate that when there's not only a lawyer but a shrink type there."

He looked back down at the paper in front of him, then up at Alice.

"And you, Officer Matthews, you up to this?"

Alice met his gaze calmly, though since I was sitting next to her, I had heard the strained but even breathing she had been doing since we'd entered the room.

"I have to be," she said.

"Yeah, yeah. You do," the captain said, and we were dismissed.

34

~

Will no one rid me of this turbulent priest?

—attributed to Henry II of England, before the death of Thomas Becket, the Archbishop of Canterbury

ADELAIDE STUCK HER HEAD in my open door. She already had her winter coat on with a huge wool shawl around her shoulders.

"Kristin, I need to make a stop across campus before we see the president," she said briskly. "I'll meet you at the president's office." And she bustled away as only she could, like she had those AI "Moonwalkers" on that I'd read about in *Wired,* a device that could make you walk faster. Before I could get my 'okay' out, she was already down the first flight of stairs.

I looked at my watch. We had half an hour until the meeting, but I wanted to fill Nia in on what I knew of the president before we got there.

I got my own coat, locked my door, and tapped on hers.

"Who is it?"

"Kristin."

"Do we need to leave already?" Nia asked as she opened the door.

"Well, Adelaide's already left. She had an errand on the way, she said. I thought we might walk slowly, and I can fill you in on what I know about this president and my impressions of him."

"Good idea," she said, reaching over for a coatrack near the door and grabbing a sleek, black, three-quarters length coat and her purse.

"So, do you know what Dr. Winters is planning for this meeting?" she asked as we descended the stairs.

"Not really, no, but since she roundly rejected 'going through channels' when I raised it, I imagine it will be some version of 'shock and awe.'"

It took our combined efforts to open the front door of Myerson against the west wind. No matter how high your down fill power was, a term I'd learned from Tom when he gave me the puffy winter coat I was wearing, the very opposite of sleek, the piercing wind with its moisture picked up from Lake Michigan could get you.

"God. Does this wind ever stop?" Nia said, turning sideways for a moment to minimize her exposure a little and turning up her generous hood.

"No, not really," I said stoically. I pulled my wool ski hat further down over my ears.

"You know, Kristin, I am on the fence about not having my lawyer at this meeting," Nia said as we walked as quickly as we could toward the building that was called, so unimaginatively, "Central Administration."

"I can see why," I said, trying to keep my teeth from chattering, "but I guess that's always an option later if this meeting is unproductive."

"I guess so," she said shivering.

"Let's duck in this building," I said, guiding her to the medieval fortress that squatted next to the concrete block of Central Administration. "They have really hot coffee and tea in the basement and some snacks if you're interested."

"Anything hot," she said as our combined efforts pushed open the huge, wooden door that had iron strapping across it. The better to keep out the marauders from Northwestern, our rival school on the north side, I thought.

We blew in the door. It was a sauna inside, and we quickly unbuttoned our coats.

Nia descended the stairs, saw a sign, and said over her shoulder, "Really, its motto actually is 'Where God drinks coffee'?"

"Yes," I said chuckling. "Never let it be said the Divinity School lacks hubris."

We quickly got our coffees, and I led her down the hall to where there were some private study cubicles. I did not want to be overheard describing the president.

The coffee was indeed hot, and we took a few, careful sips.

"So, this president, Roger Elliot Anderson, is fairly new, perhaps a year into his tenure," I said. "Anderson was only formally hired in early summer last year as his nomination had been very controversial. The presidential search itself had been contentious, at least from what I read in the university newspaper. It cost about $200,000.

"An outside search firm found this guy with an M.B. A. from Wharton with no academic experience and no administrative experience."

"Oh, how typical," Nia said. "The university website kind of fudges that, I think."

"Oh, yes. And he is supposed to be rich, I guess on the theory that somebody with money knows how to attract money. Anderson made his money in the dot com revolution, I think, but then had done other business ventures that I can't recall."

Nia chuckled. "Very memorable C.V."

"Well, you can see how Boards of Trustees these days who are mostly from that world as well would pick one of their own. I assume they thought they would get 'control' and 'success-oriented results' and so forth and no more of these messy, conflicting ideas and demonstrations on campus."

"So, you said you've met him. What's he really like?"

I considered.

"I think he's a lightweight, really. The issue Aduba and I had was also cyberbullying of a sort, but since, like this time, it violated the law, the FBI quickly took over. Up to that moment the president was trying to frame it as a 'prank.'"

I looked at my watch. "I think it's best if we let Adelaide run this show. She has something in mind, I'm sure. And we better go."

There was a glass passageway between the medieval divinity building and Central Administration, and I led Nia that way. It was very chilly in the passageway, but not the bitter cold of outside.

I knew where the president's private elevator was, and we were soon at the top floor.

There was a kind of reception/guard desk right outside the elevator door. I walked up and gave the bored-looking guy sitting there our names and said we were expected. He glanced down at a sheet on his desk and just nodded. "604" he replied. Not a huge amount of security here. I knew where the office was, and that was good, as the guard gave no directions.

In fact, 604 occupied the whole half of this floor. A door down the hall was open, and as we approached, I could see the same young, Asian man, who had been an office administrator the last time I'd been here, sitting at his extraordinary desk. At least the president hadn't spent more money decorating again.

Nia halted slightly when she saw the administrator's office. It had a desk that was completely transparent. Plastic? Glass? I'd never figured that out. A huge computer monitor still took up most of the desk. Behind this clear, angular desk chair was a white, modular credenza that blended with the wall that had been painted the same flat white.

We crossed the room toward the nearly invisible desk and identified ourselves.

"Hi, I'm Henry Chu," the young man said, standing up, and speaking in a slight Chinese accent. "Go right in. President Anderson is expecting you. Dr. Winters is already there. Let me take your coats." We gave him our outer garments, and I saw Nia continuing to look around in astonishment.

I probably should have prepped Nia more for the décor in this area, I thought. It was so jarring.

"Come right in! Welcome!" the president said in his hail-fellow, well-met heartiness.

"Hello, President Anderson," I said neutrally. "This is my colleague Dr. Nia Zendaya Turner," and Nia stepped forward and shook his hand.

"What a pleasure. And the new endowed chair has gotten off with splendid success, I see."

And then, over her shoulder, he winked at me.

Oh no. Had the anonymous donation I'd made not been so anonymous after all? I'd created a trust to donate the chair, so the trust was the donor not me.

Call Anna, my brain said as I struggled to look blankly back at him. I did not reply. He frowned slightly, his well-maintained skin drooping a little into some not quite invisible lines. After 50, it's hard to hide those lines I thought, but I was seething.

He gestured us into a conference room adjacent to the office where Adelaide was already seated, a cup in front of her.

As we walked in, Nia looked in disbelief at the conference table. It was a highly polished oval of wood, with a clear glass center through which you could see little red struts running in all directions. It was disorienting.

"So, ladies, what can I do for you?" Anderson said, seating himself at the head of the table.

I thought Adelaide's head might explode, but she just said through her teeth, "That's Dr. Winters, Dr. Turner, and Dr. Ginelli, and what you can do is issue a statement right after this meeting indicating the so-called 'Free Speech' university policy has been suspended."

"Well, now, now, there's really no need to go that far, Ms., I mean Dr . . . ." Anderson sputtered.

Adelaide talked right over him.

"That policy has literally almost blown up in the university's face, the student blogger has been arrested and will certainly be charged with federal crimes. What hasn't happened yet is the university being sued because its lax and naïve approach to cyberbullying has enabled harassment, threatening behavior and dangerous hazards in the workplace."

"The policy itself does not cause these dangers," Anderson huffed. "And the young man acted on his own."

"Baloney. It's a new day, President Anderson. The cause and effect of so-called 'free speech' in a social media world is being revisited. There is a permissive message in the hate speech of these so-called blogs and posts that ratchets up the emotions of those who see and read it," said Adelaide calmly. "It has created an environment where the lure of hateful justification of violent action is magnified. It was magnified and projected on to Dr. Turner, and it clearly had near lethal consequences."

Anderson went to reply, and Adelaide held up her hand.

"No. There's no need for further excuses. By the end of the day, you need to make an announcement that that policy is suspended and that a study commission will be convened to consult on a new policy. The new policy will be more current with the challenges of cyberspace. If you don't do that, we will declare open sesame for a battery of lawyers who are just salivating with the hope that they will be selected by us," and here she gestured to Nia and me, "to sue the pants off the university. Do I make myself clear?"

"Ahem. Well, now . . ." Anderson trailed off.

"Are we clear?" Adelaide said as she stood up and leaned a little toward him.

"I will have to consult . . ."

Adelaide broke in.

"Are we clear? If not, I have several lawyers in mind to take this case." She had her phone on the table. She picked it up and waved it like she would start speed dialing lawyers right this minute.

"Fine. Fine. Maybe that policy has become a liability."

He seemed to cheer up slightly.

"Yes, certainly. That's what I'll tell the board. A liability." He made a note on a tiny pad to his right.

"Here's my card," Adelaide pushed a card over toward him along the slick surface of the table.

"Email me the statement suspending the policy by close of business today. Otherwise," and she shook the phone again, "I start my calls."

"Well, that's that then," I said. "Nice seeing you again, President Anderson. I think we'll show ourselves out."

And I need to call Anna, I thought was we marched out, find out if there has been a leak about my donation.

35

~

If you get, give. If you learn, teach.

—Maya Angelou

SH: Good to see you again.

AM: Yeah, you too.

SH: What's on your mind for today?

AM: I went to that pool. I wanted to talk to the assistant coach. My colleague hadn't done that, and I thought it was important. I breathed through it, but I had some hitches. Kept going myself, and it got better. But I was talking to her, and she just collapsed.

SH: Really? Did you get her medical help?

AM: She refused. I mean I tried and tried. Maybe I should have just called the EMT's anyway, but I wanted to you know, respect her feelings. Kind of like you do with me. I wanted to ask about that.

SH: Your instinct was good, but the person's physical condition must guide you.

AM: Well, I was just about to call them, and she came around. I drove her home. Checked on her by cell later. She seemed okay.

SH: Tough decision. Sounds like the right one. Remember you're always free to call me.

AM: Yeah. Yeah. Thanks. It was tough. Really tough seeing her like that. I kept thinking that could be me. Has been me, though she's more of a flight response person.

SH: Everyone responds differently.

AM: Yeah, yeah, they do. (Pause)

AM: The thing is, and I need you to tell me about confidentiality here. If I tell you something about what she said is that also protected?

SH: Yes. Unless you tell me differently, it is.

AM: Well, basically she witnessed the murder. And she's going to need to testify. Even when I think of her being interviewed by those cops and me too, I guess since she told me, I feel that cold tingling like I want to freeze and forget it all.

SH: Do you have ideas how that can be made less scary?

AM: Well, yeah. Or anyway my colleague is working on it. Gettin' a lawyer for her to be with her when she talks to the cops. And maybe a therapist to be there. You know, in case it is too much for her. Problem is, those cops are gonna see her as a suspect, and they hate having therapists in interviews.

SH: Tell me about it. They really do.

AM: So, my question is, could you do that?

SH: I think that's not the best plan. I'd like to recommend someone I know is good and have her do that. There's a conflict if I'm your therapist, at least potentially.

AM: Okay then. Give me that name and contact info.

SH: I'll do that as you leave. Let's check in about you. What would you like to discuss about you?

AM: Well, I'm sleeping better but I do dream and then wake up all cold. Hard time going back to sleep. And I have zip interest in food. Jim is actually on me about it. I've lost weight, though I don't think that's such a bad thing. (Chuckles while she pats her hip).

SH: For a while maybe not, but we'll need to watch it if it becomes chronic.

AM: Sure. And work's good. We know who did the murder, we know why, and now we just have to get the bastard arrested without hurting another victim. Or really, hurting her more. I feel anxious about that, I really do, but I'm also feeling good about getting that information. And I think it's going to be helpful to her as she works it through. I've talked to her about getting into therapy. Of course, that must seem scary to her.

SH: Totally understandable.

AM: Well, it is scary at first.

SH: You can do a good job reassuring her.

36

The principle of self-defense, even involving weapons and bloodshed, has never been condemned, even by Gandhi.

— **Martin Luther King, Jr.**

"**Hey, Anna, thanks for** calling back."

"No problem at all. I do have a lawyer's name for you who is willing represent Ms. Parkinson in an interview with the police," she said in her smooth as silk voice, and she dictated the contact information to me.

"I'll give this to Alice. Alice has been our contact with the assistant coach, and she has also gotten the name and contact information for a therapist who would volunteer to be at the interview," I said.

I paused.

"Was there something else?" Anna asked as the silence lengthened.

"A couple of things."

"Well, what? Not like you to dither, Kristin," she said.

I told her about the university president winking at me when Nia, Adelaide and I had been in his office. I was concerned he knew about the money behind the trust.

"The university lawyers had to sign off on the source of those funds, but it is to be kept strictly confidential. Do you want me to follow up with them?"

"Yes, I do. I won't pull the funds, of course, but they need to know keeping that confidential is crucial if they want to get any more."

"Yes, exactly," she said.

"Another thing is I'm just not sure if Alice should be the point of contact between the witness, the lawyer, the therapist, and the police. Couldn't that increase her own risk of still being considered a suspect?"

"I suggest that you let the new lawyer handle that. It's what we do. I know you worry about your friend, but I think since she's basically cracked your case, you can trust her to carry it to the finish line."

I sighed. I did want to meddle, it was true.

"Okay then, I'll pass this along."

"Excellent," Anna said. "What about that dreadful university policy on free speech? Did that get pulled?"

"Yes, and wow. Adelaide Winters did a wonderful job of scaring the president half to death. I know she had emailed you about being one of the lawyers to threaten him if she needed to go the full distance on that."

"No problem at all. I greatly appreciate Dr. Winters and her straightforward manner."

"I do too," I chuckled.

"Babies okay?" she asked in her capacity as honorary aunt.

And we switched to discussing how they were eating and the amount of tummy time.

"And they do spend a lot of time when they're awake looking at each other. That's new," I said.

Anna praised the intelligence of the girls, as I knew she would, and then we hung up.

I sighed and leaned back. I had called Anna from my office and now I reached for the phone again to call Alice.

There was a brisk knock on the door.

We were all keeping our doors locked, of course.

"It's me, Alice. Open up, will you?" she called impatiently.

"Sure. Be right there," I said and hurried over to let her in.

"Come on in," I said. "Can I get you any coffee or tea?"

"Nah. I'm good. I need the name and contact information for that new lawyer if you've got it. I'm going to see Amanda in a little while. We're meeting at the coffee shop. I wanted to give that to her if you have it."

"Yes, I do. Have a seat while I get it," I said moving around behind my desk.

Alice groaned the moment she sat down, and she rose again immediately.

"That is a crap chair, Kristin," she said looking down at it in disbelief.

"Oh, sorry. I keep that there to deter students from getting too comfortable and deciding to tell me their life story."

I started back around the desk to get her one from Sandra's cubicle.

"No. You get me that info. I'll get a chair," she said briskly, and she pulled Sandra's desk chair over, kicking the other chair out of the way and seating herself.

I dictated the information to her, and she wrote it in her small notebook.

"So, you think she'll go through with it?" I asked. "I mean, agree to see the cops. It's a really scary thing to do when you've been hurt like she has," I said slowly, watching Alice's face.

She grimaced. The new lines in her face were still there.

"No kidding," she replied. "But yeah, I think she'll do it especially if she can have the therapist there too. You know, she's already seen that therapist once and called me to say she liked her. Amazing to me. When I think about how I had to nearly be a frozen corpse to be willing to do that. I guess they're different about that, these younger folks. Just accept talkin' to a counselor like it's not such a big deal. I think my Mama would have preferred bein' boiled in that oil my Daddy used to cook the turkey in than talk to someone about what she considered private."

"It's true, Alice," I said thinking of my own mother and her chronic addictions.

I looked at Alice. She was definitely thinner, but the animation was back in her eyes. She was sitting up straight, especially in the more comfortable chair. In fact, I thought overall she looked better than I had seen her in years. Then I saw she was considering me too.

"I am better. I know it," she said softly. "And you, you look almost like yourself too. Well," she chuckled, "except for those boobs. You never had boobs before."

"Yes, true," I said with a smile. "Tom definitely likes them."

"Well, men, you know," Alice said.

Alice left, and I shoveled paperwork around and then moved on to deleting emails. The never-ending tasks of academia. At least there were no death threats in the correspondence.

I saw it was starting to get dark even at 4:30 in the afternoon. Also, my large boobs were starting to feel taut. I needed to feed the girls. I shut down my computer and got my puffy coat.

I hurried east along with the other university toilers, but then when I turned on to our small side street, I was alone. Not many of these big Victorians were located that close to campus.

Our big, front porch had a bay window that created an alcove by the big front door. It was very dark in that space, and then I saw that the porch light over the front door was out.

No. It was broken. There was glass all over the porch.

"Don't make a move or I'll slit your throat and then go kill those kids of yours," a harsh voice said right in my ear. I felt an arm go around my chest from the left and the prick of a knife at my throat from the other hand.

"Take it easy," I said calmly. "I'll do as you say." I quietly let my purse fall to the porch floor from my right hand so I could have both hands free.

"I want those boxes. They're mine. They're mine. You stole them from me, and I want them back."

Ah. Congressional candidate Cook. He really was kind of unhinged.

"Yes. Fine. I have them in the basement around the back," I said slowly. We can go there and get them. Where did you park your car?"

His breathing became more ragged.

"I need them. I told the priest I have them. You can't lie to a priest, you know? I have to get them."

There was actual spittle sprinkling down between my puffy coat collar and my neck. The arm he had wrapped around me from the back was now shaking like palm branches in a hurricane. The knife hand was actually wobbling around. Not a good thing, actually, but I realized he was now barely holding on to me.

"We'll get them. Not a problem. Just come with me," I said, trying for the same quiet, calm tone. It wasn't easy. This guy was nuts.

I gently eased myself sideways and forward to create some distance between my neck and the knife. He didn't pull me back. I moved forward again.

Suddenly, he flew sideways and over the porch railing on the left.

"You okay, Kristin?" Kelly asked.

Apparently, she had used a side punch to throw him off the porch when I had moved so the knife was not at my throat.

"Wow. Nice work, Kelly," I said. "Those years of your taking Tae Kwon Do with me and the boys have really paid off."

"You bet," she said as we both peered over the railing. The candidate was flat on his back on the ground. His eyes were closed. He seemed to have had the wind knocked out of him.

"Well, let's go tie him up," Kelly added matter-of-factly.

"Yes, good idea," I said, a little stunned.

I picked up my purse and got out my cell phone as Kelly hurried down to tie up Cook. I called the campus police and after I'd given my address, I let them know a knife-wielding assailant had attacked me at my front door. They said they'd send a car immediately. I hung up.

I looked down off the porch. Kelly had already kicked the knife away and flipped Cook over.

Hurrying down to where they were, I unzipped my puffy coat and pulled off my belt.

We got Cook secured just as two campus cop cars screeched up.

"Kristin, you okay?" Alice called from the open door of one of the cars as she was getting out.

"Yes, Alice," I called back. "Kelly did most of the work."

I smiled down at her. She was just finishing securing Cook's hands behind him with my belt.

Alice and Mel hustled up as did two officers I didn't recognize from the next car.

"Well, hell," Alice said looking down at the trussed-up man.

I looked down at him too. Hell was fitting. Cook seemed to think the boxes of complaints he'd suppressed were sort of bundles of sin. He may have dragged them around as a penance and then, when they were gone, told the priest. He seemed to think he needed his boxes of sins to be absolved. Religion can really mess with people's heads, I thought.

I shook off those thoughts and turned to Alice.

"Alice, meet congressional candidate Cook though I doubt he'll be a candidate much longer given all that's happened."

"That's about right," she said dryly. "Let's get him arrested then," and she turned as one of the city cop cars pulled up.

"Kristin! Kelly! What's going on?" Tom called as he hurried up the sidewalk.

"Well, Tom, our daughter is a hero," I said, smiling at Kelly as she stood by the torso of the downed man making sure he didn't try to jump up.

"Oh," Tom said breathily.

"Well, this jerk threatened my mom and my sisters," she said firmly to her dad. "There's no way I was going to stand for that."

Alice walked over and patted Tom on the arm.

"Yes, Dr. Tom, there's two of them," she said with a chuckle.

37

Really good stories can help people heal.

—Susan Thistlethwaite

"**Scandal on the Southside!** Congressional Candidate and Campaign Manager Arrested!" ran the inch high headline in the *Chicago Tribune's* afternoon online edition.

The news story was reasonably accurate, I was surprised to see. "Candidate Steven William Cook who was running in the primary to replace long-time Congresswoman Beverly Ellen Hopkins who is retiring, and his campaign manager Christopher Harrison Bentley, have both been arrested on separate charges. Bentley is being held without bond in the murder of university swimming coach Harold Matthew Larsen. Cook was arrested in an attempted assault on a Hyde Park woman."

Well, that was that. Amanda Parkinson came through on her witness statement, and Alice was off the hook. Of course, Amanda would have to testify at Bentley's trial, but that was a ways off. I would have to testify about Cook holding me at knifepoint, but that was also in the future, assuming Cook chose to go to trial rather than plea bargain.

Tom and I volunteered, with the agreement of Carol, Giles, and Kelly, to take Shawna for a weekend so Alice and Jim could get away by themselves. And so, for two days we had five kids to entertain. It was frankly a circus. Thank heavens when I had offered Mrs. Brown a nanny position for at least the next three years she had said yes.

Jane came over the following week by appointment to help plan the girls' baptism. I was surprised when the boys asked if they could help us plan, and it seemed they wanted to have a role in the ceremony. Jane handled it well and asked them if they would like to be the ones to say the girls' full names when she asked. They liked that a lot.

A few days later, after things had calmed down at home, Tom and I rented a hotel room downtown at the Four Seasons. We took no luggage as we did not plan to stay overnight. But we had a nice room service dinner, and we talked without interruption about our hopes and dreams, and our concerns and deepest fears about this new and startlingly large family we now had. But mostly we talked about what we hoped for from each other. We didn't entirely resolve the tension about my pursuing investigations, but we made some progress. We also did take advantage of the remarkably large bed in the remarkably large and strangely quiet room with floor to ceiling windows that let the lights of the city illumine us as we lay on the bed together.

As spring semester rolled around, I began teaching a long-time favorite course of mine, "The New Social Gospel." Our country was being torn apart by those who saw community as including only certain white Christians. I was going week to week on revising the lectures, as so much had changed even in a few short years.

In addition, Alice, Mel, and I spent time each week in my basement making notes from Cook's boxes of ignored complaints. I had asked Alice's lawyer if anything could be done after all this time, and he had consulted some other lawyers about it. With the names and contact information it might be possible, he had said, under the new law, to do something if the complainants would be willing to file a class action suit against USA Swimming in Illinois.

We searched for the current contact information and then reached out to each of them. It was turning out many of them would like to pursue a lawsuit. We followed up with interviews that were routinely heart-breaking.

Months later we had our class action suit ready to go.

I thought about all the young people, boys and girls, who might read about such a suit and find the courage to report if they had been abused.

It would matter.

Recommended Reading

TRAUMA

Judith Herman, *Trauma and Recovery: The Aftermath of Violence--from Domestic Abuse to Political Terror* (Basic Books, 1997).

Judith Herman, *Truth and Repair: How Trauma Survivors Envision Justice* (Basic Books, 2023).

Robert Jay Lifton, *Home from the War: Learning from Vietnam Veterans* (Simon and Schuster, 1973).

Morgan Godvin, "How Veterans Created PTSD," JSTOR Daily (November 9, 2021). https://daily.jstor.org/how-veterans-created-ptsd/

Robert Jay Lifton: *Surviving Our Catastrophes: Resilience and Renewal from Hiroshima to the COVID-19 Pandemic* (The New Press, 2023).

Sharon Ellis Davis, *The Trauma of Sexual and Domestic Violence: Navigating My Way through Individuals, Religion, Policing, and the Courts* (Cascade Books, 2022).

ASSAULT AND SEXUAL VIOLENCE

Associated Press, "Six Women File Lawsuits Against USA Swimming Over Alleged Sexual Abuse by Coaches," (June 10, 2020).

https://www.usatoday.com/story/sports/olympics/2020/06/10/usa-swimming-women-sue-alleged-sex-abuse/5339685002/

Laura Nelson, "As Deadline Looms, California's Institutions Face a Flood of Sexual Abuse Lawsuits," *Los Angeles Times*, (December, 2022).

https://www.latimes.com/california/story/2019-10-13/child-sexual-abuse-allegations-extension-filing-allegations-california-law

Discussion Questions

1. Surviving sexual and domestic abuse and taking steps toward healing from the trauma of those experiences are the main themes of this work. As you are comfortable, what is your own experience of trauma or your observations about trauma in others? What has it taught you?
2. Pregnancy and nursing new babies are a constant presence in this mystery novel. What are your thoughts about how our society regards the biological processes of motherhood? Does our society think pregnant or lactating women can *think* much less work at full capacity?
3. There are three main trauma responses, fight, flight, or freeze. Why do you think Alice Matthews freezes when she starts to remember the sexual abuse by her swimming coach?
4. Another important theme of the novel is the nature of free speech today. Do you agree with a university policy that basically any speech is considered free speech unless it is a direct threat? What are the problems with that perspective that you can see? What do you think constitutes "incitement to harm" in speech and how should that be dealt with?
5. Before they can be destroyed, Kristin Ginelli grabs boxes of complaints about abusive swim coaches that have been hidden and ignored for many years. Was she right or wrong to do that? What were her options?
6. What is "whiteness" and how do you define it in today's society? What is the history of the social construction of whiteness as far as you know? Is that different from or similar to racism?

7. What needs to happen to protect kids, young people, and adults from sexual abuse? Should laws be changed so that such crimes can be reported even decades after the assault(s)? What is the policy in your state?

www.ingramcontent.com/pod-product-compliance
Lightning Source LLC
Chambersburg PA
CBHW070630310726
48982CB00001B/230

* 9 7 9 8 3 8 5 2 1 0 6 2 6 *